The Orchid

Jimmy Turner's life, shattered by a twist of fate, is over except that nobody told Lindsey Schnetler. This newly arrived neighbor endures Jimmy's temper, scorn and abuse with a calm fearlessness that captures Jimmy's heart. He has much to learn about life and death. When the tables turn and Lindsey's life is threatened, Jimmy has to use everything he has become to try to save her.

This story is fiction with no relationship to persons living or dead.

The Orchid
Romance

RC Waggoner

2007

The Orchid

Chapter 1

The brown-haired girl stood awkwardly in the doorway. "Your mom said it would be okay if I came up for a few minutes." She looked into my room curiously and then, just as curiously, back at me.

Closer up, I could see that she had not yet grown into her body. She was all arms, elbows and knees. She was skinny with no figure at all. Her eyes were large, flecked with green and her nose was a trifle too big to fit her face. In other words, she was rather homely. "Suit yourself." I turned and did a wheelie with the chair. She gasped thinking I was going to flip over and I smiled to myself. Girls were so naïve. With all wheels back on the ground, I returned to my puzzle and tried to make my point by ignoring her. After a few minutes, I glanced at her. She was looking at the odd assortment of memorabilia I had not thrown out yet: the football plaques, the first place ribbons from summer tennis camps and other sports trophies that littered a couple of shelves in my room. Because she thought I was ignoring her, she walked to my bookcase and peered at my collection of reading material. From there she went to the window and noticed the binoculars.

Finally, she turned and came to stand by the card table where I was assembling a thousand-piece puzzle. "Can I help you do that?"

I looked up. "No."

I saw the shock register on her face and felt guilty pleasure. I figured she would run out of the room with tears in her eyes and tell her parents what a mean boy I was.

Instead, she bit her lip. "I like puzzles," she said, valiantly ignoring my rudeness. Then she gave me a toothy grin. "I'm probably better at it than you are."

I cast a scornful glance in her direction. She endured it.

The rage inside me was not her fault. I was not mad at her in particular; I was mad at anyone who saw life through rose-colored glasses, full of "endless possibilities," and nonsense like that. Condemn them to a wheelchair for the rest of their life and see their reaction then!

"This is an adult puzzle." I stressed the word adult. "It is too difficult for little kids."

I almost smirked at the expression on her face. She was trying to be polite and I was chewing her up. I owed her nothing. She barged in on my territory. This was my sanctuary. Come in here at your own risk!

She wavered for a moment, I saw it on her face, but then she drew a deep breath. I thought she was going to give me a lecture on being nice to people and then run out. I would have deserved it, and it would have been fun to watch. Instead, she said, "You don't have to be mean." The girl picked a puzzle piece from the litter of pieces on the table and stuck it in place, "One to nothing!" Her voice wavered slightly as she met my rude stare.

"Damn it," I mumbled under my breath, low enough that she could not make out the words. She was not going to go easily. "Why the hell don't you just go back to your normal little life with all your normal little friends?" While I was mumbling, I found a piece and snapped it forcefully into place. I found five in a row and snapped them into place. She could not find any. I looked at her with pity in my eyes. "Come back when you actually *are* good at something."

I saw a tear form in one of those green-flecked brown eyes and spill over onto her cheek. She mopped it with a backhand as she studied the puzzle.

I felt bad inside, but anger does funny things to you. I found another piece and then another and finally she found one. It was seven to two when my mom came up the steps. "Your mom and dad are getting ready to go, Lindsey," she said to the girl. "I see you've met Jimmy." Lindsey studiously avoided looking at my mom. I figured it was so that my mom would not see the liquid brimming just under her lids.

Mom's brows knit as she discerned tension between us. She studied me critically, knowing that something was wrong, but not certain what I had done.

I glared back at her. There was no use pretending. I did not like my life. I could not find any reason to pretend I was happy.

❖❖❖❖❖

Nine months earlier, on a drizzly afternoon, on the way home with my mom after football practice, I saw it come out of the woods near the road just in time to yell a warning to my mom. The next few seconds lasted a lifetime. Until we hit the tree, I saw everything in super slow motion: rain, blacktop, green grass, a bush and then nothing. At fifty miles-an-hour, the car went over the shoulder, down the embankment and hit an oak. I woke up when they were loading me into the ambulance. A thick white brace surrounded my neck.

Too dizzy to focus, I heard my mom's voice and knew she was alive. I tried to open my eyes, but the swirling scenery threatened to make me hurl, so I closed them quickly hoping the nausea I felt was temporary. I heard my mom begging me to squeeze her fingers so I tightened my fist. The rest of the way to the hospital she was sobbing with relief and apologizing.

I heard the word paralysis, and the phrase "spinal cord injury suspected" as the medic attending me in the back of the ambulance talked to mom and someone on the radio. I prayed that it was not my mom who was paralyzed. I was certain I was not the one because, other than my head, I felt fine. I suspected I had a concussion and that is why I felt nauseous and dizzy. Then I decided I was feeling that way because of the hard surface of the gurney or the solid undercarriage of the ambulance. It felt like the thing had no shock absorbers. I felt every bump in my shoulders and head.

When the medic had done all he could, mom took my hand and held it. I managed to open my eyes. Mom was sitting on the bench next to me. Her eyes studied me worriedly out of a face streaked with tears. She kept glancing at my feet or legs with such a sad expression on her face that I got worried.

"What happened, mom?"

"I should have hit that deer," mom said. Her voice choked with the threat of new tears. "I shouldn't have swerved!" She was crying again. "I'm so sorry, Jimmy! I'm so very sorry!"

"We didn't hit anyone did we?" I asked.

"No, Jimmy."

"Then who's paralyzed?"

She burst into fresh tears and I caught on. I was the one! Instantly I discounted the idea: these things do not happen to my family or me. They happen to strangers and you feel sorry for them for a few minutes and then go on with your business. I felt panic in my throat like someone gripping me with a strong hand. I lifted my hand and looked at it: I could move! A sense of relief shot through me. I looked at my mom.

She was looking at my legs. I lifted a leg to show her that I was okay. Nothing happened. I reached down and felt my stomach and my hips. My hips felt funny. It seemed as though I was touching someone else's hips because I could not feel the pressure of my fingers on them. My eyes widened in fear as I looked at my mom.

The attendant saw my panic and leaned forward. "These things are often temporary," he said soothingly. "Let's wait 'till we get to the hospital. I'm going to check your pulse now."

I took comfort from his words.

Nine months later, sitting in my upstairs bedroom behind the large windows overlooking the front of our fifty acres, I thought bitterly how much my life had changed in less than five seconds.

In the intervening months in the hospital the only thing that stood out in sharp detail was the day they fitted me for my wheelchair. Surgery shortly after the accident made it possible for me to sit up and the wheelchair gave me a tiny measure of freedom and independence back. Only my mom was there for the event. Dad had to work. The male nurse helped me into the chair. I wheeled myself down the hall and then back. I was exhausted. My mom could not stop her tears.

Over the next few weeks, I gained strength and calluses until at last I was able to maneuver myself out of bed and into the wheelchair without crashing to the floor.

The day I came home, my dad took off from work to help. After what must have been a lot of debate while I was in the hospital, my parents installed an elevator. Mom was convinced that I would do better in familiar surroundings—regain at least a tiny sense of normalcy by being in my room. She was wrong about that. I hated my room, I hated the house and I hated my life.

Two or three times that first week, I contemplated suicide. I rode my prison wagon to the top of the stairway and debated the best way to end it: would the stairs break my neck or not? Would I suffer even more by becoming quadriplegic? That question stopped me every time. I could not bear to lose the little bit of my life that remained if it did not work.

I saw it as a blessing when my so-called friends stopped visiting and calling. I hated them anyway. They could walk. They were insensitive. They did not know how to talk about anything but football, sports and girls. I did not have a girl friend. I liked some girls but never had the courage to talk to them. Now I decided it was a good thing.

My anger grew daily as I watched the sun come up on a world that still grew green grass and go down on a world that had no interest in me. My parents did not count. They were required by virtue of their roles to have an interest. Sorry, that was just the way it was. They were obligated to care for me. I did not hate them but I was so angry about the unfairness of life that I took it out on anyone who came around. My mom spent less and less time trying to cheer me up and my dad found reasons to stay at work longer and longer each day.

I was oblivious to the damage I was inflicting because I hated everything and everyone so intensely. As the days went by, I found myself grinding my jaws and poking stickpins into my arms just to feel the pain.

My parents gave up getting me to go back to Cross Field High School. They brought psychiatrists and social workers and even went so far as to bring a preacher from a local church to talk to me but it did not help. My anger only grew more intense. When I turned sixteen, I did not legally have to go to school and sixteen was close enough now that any attempt to force me to go would result in open rebellion.

It did not change my heart one bit when I heard my mom crying in the kitchen as she worried about me. As far as I was concerned, my future was dead so I might as well be dead too. The psychiatrist tried to give me hope by telling me about people who, despite their wheelchairs, made a difference. I was not buying that crap. I wallowed in self-pity because it felt better than attempting to start over now that everything I used to be good at was no longer possible.

Somewhere in the middle of my self-pity, mom talked me into writing how I felt. I did it when the boredom of my inactivity became too great to endure. A small magazine published the article. I got a few letters from some sympathetic folks. My mom framed the article and hung it in my room.

My mom and dad tried to interest me in video games but I could not focus on them long enough to get good. They tried to read to me but I ignored them. One day my mom brought a box up and laid it on the card table just inside my room. After she left, I wheeled away from my semi-permanent pity perch at the window and looked at the box. It was a puzzle with 1,000 pieces. For a week, I ignored it and then one day spilled the pieces onto the table and began to put the puzzle together. I think I did it because I was so bored that I had to do something. Soon it became a challenge to see how fast I could fit the pieces together. I did not admit it but when mom brought up harder ones, I was pleased. I began to challenge myself to start and finish a puzzle in one day. I could do it alone, so it allowed me to remain angry at the world while feeling some measure of satisfaction in beating the puzzle. At least I could put a puzzle together when I could not do that with my life. When I got bored with puzzles, I picked up a book—one of the dozen that mom brought up and just left in my room—and began to read. Louis L'Amour soon captured my attention. Mom happily brought me everything he wrote—which was a lot!

The distance that developed between my parents and me is the result of my attitude. I cannot help the way I feel about things. They do not agree, so they constantly try to tell me how good life could be if I just give it a chance. They see life a lot rosier than I do. My mom tries her best to convince me that life can go on and should. It makes it hard to talk to them.

Another thing that was difficult was finding out that the people who were my best friends found it easy to abandon me. They did not know what to say to me. They felt awkward and uncomfortable. Pity only takes you so far. Friendship cannot survive pity.

I hate going out in public. When I do leave the house for a doctor's appointment or because I cannot stand to look at these four walls for another minute, and roll down the sidewalk in my wheelchair, I am the person everyone pities.

Chapter 2

I knew who the brown-haired girl was even though I did not know her name.

Our house is a Victorian, two-story with the traditional columns and massive doors. My bedroom window overlooks the front of our fifty-acre property. To the right I can see the next-door neighbor's house. It had been vacant from before my accident. A month ago, I heard a car alarm beeping. From the upstairs window, I saw a realtor showing a family through the house. One of my dad's security devices must have triggered their car alarm or they accidentally triggered it themselves.

I was about to wheel away from the window and go back to my puzzle when I saw a young girl step out of the house and look around the yard. I reached for my binoculars and peered through them. The girl was probably ten or eleven years old with short brown hair and, from that distance, a decent face. I watched the activity for a while until the family and the realtor got into their cars and drove away. Disappointed with the lack of entertainment, I put the binoculars down and returned to my puzzle.

Two weeks ago, I watched a moving van discharge its load of furniture and figured out that someone had purchased that house next door. Not that it mattered to me. I observed for a little while to see who was moving in. My binoculars were powerful and at that distance, about 300 yards, it brought things in sharp and clear. The girl I had seen two weeks earlier filled my vision as she climbed out of a station wagon and walked into the house. The whole time she walked, she looked almost right at me! It freaked me out. I knew it was impossible for her to see me from that distance inside my room, behind double-thick glass, but she seemed to be looking right at me anyway. She had a clear complexion, a bit pasty white for this part of the country. I focused briefly on the license plate of the station wagon. Massachusetts. Oh well, perhaps she would find it easier to get sun in Tennessee. I watched until my arms ached but saw nothing else of interest. At least it beat putting puzzles together.

During the intervening two weeks, I saw a flurry of activity at the house but eventually lost interest.

I was working on a puzzle when our doorbell rang. A minute later, the intercom startled me. "Jimmy!" My mom tends to holler when she really does not need to. The intercom works just fine at normal voice levels. Somehow, she does not get the electronic stuff. Maybe Alexander Graham Bell had to yell at Watson just in case the telephone did not work, who knows. My mom might as well as have yelled at me from the bottom of the steps.

I sighed and wheeled over to the box. "What?" Yeah, I was rude, so what? I did not feel like being put on display for our new neighbors. What would it accomplish? Someone else to pity me? No thanks.

Mom tried to keep her voice neutral, even though she correctly interpreted my rudeness. "Our new neighbors, the Andersons, have come for a visit. Please come down."

I flipped the switch off and glared at it. "Right," I said. "Like that's going to happen." Fifteen minutes later, there was a light tap at my door. It would be my mom, trying to be polite but firm to avoid embarrassing our guests. It would not be right for them to hear her getting angry with her handicapped son. I almost ignored it. Still, it would serve little purpose to make my mom look bad in front of our neighbors by being completely rude—maybe there was a little spark of humanity left in me. At least I could give her an excuse with which she could save face. I owed her that much so I wheeled to the door and opened it.

That put me eye-to-eye with the brown-haired neighbor girl.

Tension filled the room as I glared at my mom, but Lindsey studied me calmly as if trying to decide how to ignore my rudeness. She spoke first to my mom. "I did meet him," she said pleasantly. Apparently, in that short space of time, she figured out what to say to me. She looked me in the eye, "This wasn't enough time to have a real contest."

I thought she was making excuses and grinned wickedly at her. "Whatever," I said, dismissing her as if she had accomplished nothing.

"Okay, then. Nice to meet you, Jimmy," Lindsey said. She was determined to be polite to the end as she backed out of the room. On the other hand, maybe she was showing off for my mother.

Inside I chalked up a score. Her innocent, ordinary view of life without problems angered me. I did not invite her to come up to my room anyway; my mom must have sent her up. I doubted my mom would make that mistake again!

I waved as if shooing her out of the room and caught an evil glare from my mom before she followed Lindsey down the stairs. I was not worried about my mom yelling at me. She had not scolded me since the accident. I hated that things were absolutely *not* normal but I was just angry enough to take advantage of it too. After Lindsey left, I felt my conscience talking to me. I wondered if I felt bad or if

I did not care. I couldn't tell. The thought caused me to catch my breath.

At noon the next day, my mom yelled into the intercom that Lindsey was here. I should come down. I flipped the intercom off and stayed in bed. Ten minutes later the girl knocked at the door. I ignored her. I heard her go back down the steps. The anger inside of me was satisfied. Soon my mom came up and, more forcefully than she had said anything to me in the last year, told me that I was being rude. She made me get out of bed and get dressed. I grudgingly did it because I was surprised at my mom's anger. When I was dressed and in my chair, mom stuck her head in the door and told me she was sending Lindsey up.

"What for?" I asked brusquely, determined to exact a measure of revenge for her forcing me to do something I did not want to do.

"Don't be rude!" My mom warned me. She waited until Lindsey came in the room to make sure I was going to be civil. I could tell she was reluctant to leave Lindsey alone with her horrible son.

Lindsey stepped into the room. "Hi, Jimmy."

"Hi." I glowered back. I spoke only because my mom was still there.

Mom gave me a steady look that was a warning and an expression of disbelief that I would treat anyone as poorly as I was treating Lindsey. When I looked away, feeling slightly ashamed, she walked out.

Lindsey idly brushed her hair from her eyes and tucked it behind one ear with her index finger. "I'm ready for the contest again, Jimmy." She looked resolutely at me.

I glared at her. My mom chose that moment to return and stick her head in the door. "Jimmy, I'm making soup and sandwiches for lunch. Lindsey said she will not mind bringing yours up so I will call you when they are ready." She reached over and flipped the intercom's switch to ON. She gave me another warning look that said she caught my ugly look at Lindsey and did not want that repeated before she went down the stairs.

"I hope you're not mad at me for coming over," Lindsey said slowly.

"What would give you that idea?" I asked sarcastically.

"Well, you just seem mad." She looked at me with eyes that were a richer brown color. The flecks of green were still there. Her face was clear, innocent, and happy. It annoyed me to see her so cheerful. She knew nothing of real hurt, pain, or anguish.

"Your powers of deduction are amazing," I said clipping each word.

"I don't understand," Lindsey's eyebrows knitted together. The effect was slightly comical.

I laughed. Her face registered alarm and then cautious amusement. She really did not know how to take me. When she smiled, I saw a row of fresh adult teeth that had adolescent gaps between each tooth. She had not yet gotten all her teeth because nothing in that mouth was crowded. Her teeth were slightly off-white and a little crooked and for some reason that softened me. She was not perfect. I looked at her. It made her uncomfortable. She did not appear to be intimidated, just awkward. Maybe she was not here because she pitied me or wanted to help me. However, the longer I looked at her with the question of *why are you here*, the harder it was to guess. Suddenly I felt bad that I was being so mean. I sighed, "Sit."

She pulled a chair over from the desk and sat down at the card table. "I'm ready if you are."

Her persistence had its effect. I shrugged and pulled my

crip-mobile up to the card table. I actually got interested in beating her, and when my mom called up fifteen minutes later, we had a fourth of the puzzle done. She found as many pieces as I had. I could feel the thrill of competition running through my veins for the first time in a long time. I was secretly amazed at how good she was.

Lindsey retrieved lunch from down stairs and put it on the card table, covering up the puzzle with the tray. While we ate, I noticed that she wiped her mouth with the back of her sleeve. I thought that was just right. It fit my mood. It was against the rules, whatever they were, and here was a ten or eleven year old girl who wiped soup off her mouth with her sleeve. Fascinating!

"You seem happier," she said after finishing her meal.

"Maybe I am." I decided being churlish was not as much fun as competing with her had been. Plus, she refused to be intimidated or insulted.

Lindsey burped and looked at me with that half-embarrassed look that could turn into total embarrassment if I acted shocked. I grinned and burped louder. Her eyes narrowed and the corners of her lips turned up in a slight smile as she realized this too was a competition. Refusing to be outdone, she reached way down, pulled one up, and let it fly just as my mom stepped into the room behind her.

I laughed so hard I almost fell out of the wheelchair. My mom just looked at Lindsey's back, not certain she had done it, but pretty sure I hadn't because she had been looking at me. Very quietly, she backed out of the room. I know she was hoping that Lindsey would never know she had come in at that most awkward moment. The sight was too much for me and I laughed so hard I nearly choked. When I could no longer catch my breath, I had to stop and recover. Lindsey was looking at me with the look of someone who has triumphed rather than embarrassed herself so I guessed she did not know my mom had stepped into the room just as she belched.

Lindsey thought the first one was funny so she reached down, dredged up another one, and let it fly. Grudging admiration welled up inside me. It was hard to believe that a girl knew how to belch by dragging air into her gut and reversing the flow like that. It was also harder to believe that she would do it.

"Damn, Lindsey!" She was quite satisfied with herself and knew she had won our impromptu contest until I giggled and pointed at the door. "My mom heard that!" The memory overwhelmed me as much as her reaction to what I had just told her and I laughed as much this time as I did before.

Her face turned red and then pink as she absorbed the idea that my mom had heard her do something very unladylike just moments earlier and that she might have heard the second one too. She covered her mouth with her hand and looked at me wide-eyed. She glanced at the door before she said with a giggle, "My dad taught me how to do that before he died."

It was my turn to sober. "I thought your dad just came over yesterday."

"My real dad," she said. She gave me a serious look. "That's my step dad. My mom married him three weeks ago and yuck!" She grinned at me. I looked at her until she made another face. Then I knew what she meant. She had to get out of the house because they were newlyweds.

"Not something I'll ever have to worry about," I said sourly.

She gave me the wide eyes and said in a whisper, "You mean your mom and dad don't do it?"

I could not help but admire her quick-witted response. She knew I did not mean that but she got me anyway because I responded, "No. I meant *I* won't have to worry about that."

She felt guilty for saying it and my response caused her face to turn red when she understood. She picked up the tray to cover her embarrassment and said, "I guess I'll take the dishes downstairs. I can come back up if you want me to."

"Up to you," I said. If I said I wanted her to come back, it would look like I was lonely. I did not want her pity. I had lived on anger for so long that I was not ready to give that up yet. I did not want to be her friend until she made friends with kids her own age, leaving me to sit in my wheelchair watching life through the window again. I realized there was a tiny spark of hope in me that maybe someone *wanted* to spend time with me because that someone found me interesting and likeable rather than someone to pity. I could not afford to admit to myself that I hoped she came back.

Lindsey looked hurt and started to say something but then decided to bite her tongue. When she walked out, the room felt empty. She came back the next day and put up with my crap for a couple of hours before she had to go home. I gave her a ton of crap too because unconsciously I was trying to see if she thought I was worth the effort. It was self-destructive behavior. To my surprise, she was persistent and came back the next day and the next. I was starting to feel a little safer—like maybe she was the one who wanted to come over when I had a chilling thought. Maybe my mom was putting her up to it. Worse yet, what if someone was paying her to come over every day, just to get me interested in life again? I could not help it; my teeth ground together in anger because that suddenly seemed logical.

I went down the elevator and wheeled out into the kitchen where mom was baking. She heard me roll through the doorway. She turned and her eyes brightened until she saw my expression. Still, she asked if I wanted a cookie even while she braced herself. I took one.

With my mouth full I said, "How much are you paying Lindsey to come over here everyday?"

She nearly dropped her cookie sheet. "What?" Then she got mad. "You just say anything that pops into your head. It's a wonder that sweet girl comes back at all!" She glared at me.

When I did not answer, she sat down at the table and looked at me. "You're afraid, aren't you?"

"No!" I said and wheeled out of the room before she could ask more questions.

I had my answer, but I still could not figure out why she was coming over. I also knew she would soon make other friends and I would be history. I spent a lot of time that night trying to figure out why she was coming over and how to get her to admit her reasons.

The next day she came over, happy and bubbly. We worked on the puzzle and after half an hour, finished it. She put the last piece in place and smiled triumphantly at me. "We did it!"

I nodded. "So now you can quit coming," I said bluntly.

She looked up startled, but her expression told me that she was not sure if I was bluffing. "Why? Are you afraid I'm better than you at this?"

That challenge threatened to derail my plan. "I'm not

afraid of that," I replied before realizing that she had gotten me off track. "That's not the point!" I wheeled my chair away from the table and turned it toward her. "Why are you coming over here? Taking pity on a poor invalid boy?"

"No." The question seemed to throw her off balance, but only for a moment. She shrugged her shoulders. "I just have to get out of the house sometimes."

"So go to the park!" I was angry. Coming over here was just a convenient escape from her house! It confirmed my darkest thoughts. When she had better friends, I would be off her list.

She stood angrily, knocking the chair over in the process. She bent and picked it up and apparently came to some conclusion during that time. "I will go to the park if you tell me you don't want me to come back here!" Her hands moved up to her hips and she looked at me with a mixture of anger and worry.

"You're ten friggin' years old!" I wheeled my chair around to face her. "I'm fifteen. Maybe you better grow up."

She stared at me. "I'm not ten." Then she grinned—fully recovered from her worry in that two second space of time—and let just a touch of sarcasm lace her words. "And I don't see any other people knocking your door down!" I think my mouth dropped open. I was so angry for a minute that I actually felt my vision narrowing. So mad, in fact, that I could not form a response that seemed appropriate. Anything not appropriate would make me feel, and look, like a fool. She waited, ready to continue the battle if I were stupid enough. She knew she had drawn first blood. I could not think of an appropriate response. She started pulling the puzzle apart and dropping the pieces in the box.

"Fuck off!" I said in frustration. I kept my voice down in case mom was listening on the intercom.

"Jimmy! You shouldn't cuss like that!" She was teasing now, and *not* afraid of my anger. She had begun taking the puzzle apart and now she pulled more pieces off the puzzle and dropped them in the box, ignoring me.

I hated it when someone ignored me. When you live in a wheelchair, people ignore you because they do not know what to say around you. That is a huge insult. I knew she was not insulting me but I could not stop the anger that bubbled out of me full of insecurity and fear. "Damn it, Lindsey!" I wheeled my chair and went to the window. With my back to her I raged, "That's your fucking house!" I pointed. "I don't need any babies to hold my hand! Just get the fuck out of here!"

I expected her to burst into tears and run out of the room. Instead, I heard her emit a stifled giggle. I wheeled around, very annoyed, until I saw my mom with the tin of cookies in her hand and a look of shock on her face. She put the tin down on the card table and gently said, "You might want to go home for now, Lindsey. Jimmy and I need to talk." There was polished steel in her tone and her eyes bored into me like daggers.

A slight shiver crawled up my backbone. I was in trouble now! When the front door closed downstairs, my mom turned her wrath on me. "Jimmy! I should wash your mouth out with soap! How dare you talk to a young girl that way! How dare you talk that way?" She was furious.

This was the mom I respected from *before* she felt guilty about the accident. "I'm sorry, mom."

"That's not good enough. Tomorrow you will apologize to that young lady! You better be grateful that someone around here is willing to put up with your attitude because your dad and I have had enough!" She stomped around the room picking up my laundry and straightening things out with many clumps and bangs. I guessed she wanted to milk her anger now that she had finally released some of it. That is why she was not leaving.

Over the last year, my mom took the brunt of my anger. She was the only one I could take my frustration and rage out on. When she heard me say those angry things to Lindsey, my mom had all she could stomach. She took the abuse I gave because she felt guilty but Lindsey had done nothing to deserve my anger.

For the first time since the accident, I felt my anger start to melt. I did not want to be angry. I did not want to keep hurting anyone who tried to get close to me. I knew it was wrong. I was relieved that my mom was finally talking to me with the kid gloves off.

I did not want to keep hurting her. I was wrong about Lindsey's reasons for coming over. I was wrong to take out my anger on my mom. The big balloon of hurt slowly started to deflate inside me. I took a deep breath and said sincerely, "I'm sorry, mom." It felt good to say it. I was sorry! A year of being angry at everything melted away. I felt clean and fresh. Hope started to fill up the reservoir previously stuffed with anger. I just could not explain it. I smiled at my mom. "I really am sorry."

She looked at me with questions and then decided I might be telling the truth. She sat down at the card table. "I'm sorry you were the one who got hurt, Jimmy. You don't know how often I've begged God to give you back your legs. It's so hard seeing you like this!" Tears began to run down her cheeks. She had held these words inside for a long, long time. Now they came bubbling out. "No parent should have to see her child..." she fumbled for the right words, could not find them so she finished, "...like this."

I did not know how to comfort her. I did not know how to live outside of my anger. It was easier to blame everyone and everything instead of moving forward. How many thousands of stunted people were there like me in this world? We couldn't move ahead because we delighted in being angry over what we had lost. It was so much easier than accepting responsibility for what we had and moving on from there.

"I love you, Jimmy." My mom had so much she wanted to say. I could see it in her eyes and yet she did not know how to say it, I guess. Finally, she came over, put her face alongside mine, and hugged the part of me she could reach in the wheelchair. After a minute, she kissed me and went downstairs.

With the departure of anger, I realized I was lonely. The longer I stayed in my room, the lonelier I got. I was so used to living in anger that it was as if a friend had suddenly left me. I was terribly lonely.

I went down the elevator and rolled into the kitchen where mom was working. "Mom, I guess I've been mad at the world and God and everyone else because of what happened. You just don't know what it's like to know you are never going to be normal!"

My mom stopped working and sat down. "It's been hard on all of us. Your dad has suffered terribly. He doesn't know how to handle it."

"I guess when we couldn't play tennis or golf anymore we just didn't have anything in common." I picked a warm cookie off the sheet and ate it.

"That's part of it," my mom said. "He didn't know how to help you. That is the biggest reason. He feels helpless to fix what happened."

I felt a rush of the old anger. "I just wish he'd talk to me sometimes," I said. The heat had come into my voice so quickly that it made me aware of how much I missed my dad. We used to do things together. "We were going to buy an old Junker and fix it up together but now..."

"Talk to him, Jimmy. Tell him these things."

"It's been so long since we talked, I don't know how."

"You'll figure it out." My mom gave me a confident smile and patted my arm.

"I'll apologize to Lindsey, mom. I shouldn't have said those things."

"I'm glad. I just hope..." she left the statement unsaid. I knew what she meant. I hope you did not hurt her feelings so much that she will not come back and our name becomes mud with our new neighbors!

I guess I could have called her to apologize but I did not want to. If she came back after today, it meant she was coming of her own free will! If her parents thought it was okay before, they would not think so now if she told them what I had said. I would be lucky if she ever thought about me again. I sighed. The bottom line was that if she came over again, it meant that she wanted to. I needed to know that. I hoped it was true. I spent a restless night tossing in my bed. It meant that much to me.

The next day, in spite of a sleepless night, I dressed early and wheeled to the window. I picked up a book so I could pretend to be reading when she arrived. I put the book down and picked it up a half dozen times. Lindsey did not come when she usually did. I peered out of the window and even searched for signs of life at her house. Maybe they went to the store. Maybe she had to do chores. Bitterness started to creep back in. My happy feelings from yesterday started to leak. My mom had to like me; Lindsey did not. The true test was Lindsey, not my mom. I turned away from the window after a half hour. I was broken hearted. I wanted to go downstairs and talk to my mom so she could comfort me or at least help me get my perspective back.

A dozen more times I went to the window. Each time I grew disgusted with my transparent need for someone to think I was worth being around and turned away only to return. Finally, I realized that I had my answer and turned away. I wanted to scatter the new puzzle pieces all over the room with one angry sweep of my hand. I hated puzzles! I hated waiting for a doorbell or a knock or a voice to say, "Hi Jimmy." Why did this happen to me? I knew I should not have gotten used to her coming over! I knew it! I ground my teeth. The room was stuffy, hot, and too small. I could not stand my room suddenly. I decided to go downstairs. All the good feelings that flowed from forgiveness left me. The hurt returned like a lump of lead in my chest.

I sensed that I was not alone and looked up. She was in the doorway. My heart gave up all of its anger as if someone had poked it with a pin. I stared at her. She looked at me. Finally, she broke the silence. "Your mom said it would be okay if I came up." She said the exact same thing to me when she braved the unknown and came to my room the first day. When I could not respond she said, "Can I come in?"

My surprise eased and I waved her into the room. Instead of coming in all the way, she leaned around the door and switched the intercom to ON and turned the volume up. I could tell she was waiting for me to speak. A suspiciously devilish look made the green in her eyes show up. I stared at her in disbelief. I was sure my mom put her up to that move! She had expertly trapped me. I took a deep breath and gave her what she was expecting. I said as quietly as I could because I knew my mom was listening downstairs,

"I'm sorry for what I said yesterday." I probably blushed because my face felt warm.

Lindsey giggled under her breath, holding her hand over her mouth so my mom could not hear it over the intercom. She struggled for a moment and then said a lot louder, "What about all the other nasty things you said to me?"

My eyes went wide. I wanted to strangle her, but I managed to croak out, "Yeah, those things too."

"I accept." She switched the intercom OFF and grinned at me triumphantly.

"You little fox!" I said. I tried to come toward her to grab her or do something to pay her back but she was faster than I was and dashed around the card table giggling. The table wiggled dangerously on its four spindly legs as she bumped it with her hip on the way around.

She kept the card table between us. "So are you going to be nicer to me now?"

"Hell no!" I kept my voice low in case my mom had come creeping up the steps when the intercom went dead. I was counting on her not coming up the steps. If I had a sister, this is exactly how she would have acted. She would have taken advantage of the moment to pay me back. I could feel the steam boiling.

"Good. I like you just like that." She sat down and grinned at me.

The heat dropped. The steam evaporated. "You what?"

"I like you all crazy mean like that," she clarified. She was watching me like a hawk lest I suddenly dash in her direction with my crip-mobile. One never knew what a crazy mean person would do.

"Crazy mean..." I stopped thinking about retribution. She really did have guts, humor, and smarts. I leaned back to show that I had given up my desire to exact revenge. I studied her face and then her body—as much as I could see above the card table. I finally asked the question that had been bugging me. "Just how old are you?"

"How old do you think?"

"Oh, five, maybe six years old at the most," I grinned maliciously at her.

She gave me a disgusted look mixed with humor. She knew I was joking and that I probably did not have a clue as to her real age. "Twelve." Then she smiled sweetly and said, "At least I will be next week!"

"That's not much older than ten!" I said trying to salvage my ego.

"It's quite a bit older," she said disagreeing with me. "Truce?" She held her hand up, palm toward me.

"Not a..." I looked at her and the doorway suspiciously, "...friggin' chance."

"Friggin's okay to say," she giggled. Then she leaned toward me and whispered conspiratorially, "But not the other stuff you say like fucking or shit." Then her face broke into a bright red flame and she giggled guiltily. I got the feeling that she was trying hard to impress me. She wanted me to like her. That thought hit me like a clap of thunder. I was so busy wanting people to like me and not pity me that the realization she wanted me to like her almost left me speechless.

I had to catch my jaw before it fell off my face. "Is it okay if I use the occasional damn?" I tried to recover before she realized she was outsmarting me.

"As long as your mom doesn't hear you," she replied with a satisfied grin.

I had to admit to myself: She had just won the second round. I never had a little sister but damn if she would not have been a good one. You get mad at little sisters but love, and hate them all in the same ten minutes. "Truce," I capitulated.

After Lindsey left, I sat gazing out the window as the sky went dark. The lights in her house glowed with life. I could not see her room but she told me she had the upstairs bedroom and loved it because she could see the same things from her window that I saw from mine. The grass seemed greener, like it does after a shower. The air smelled fresher and my room did not seem as small and cramped as it had earlier. Why? What changed? How could my room get larger, my bed more comfortable, my chair less of a burden and the grass greener just like that?

⋅⋰⋅∗⋅⋰⋅∗⋅⋰⋅

A few weeks went by and we put together every puzzle I had. She was good at it and I enjoyed the competition. I decided to teach her the game of chess. She learned quickly and soon I was fighting for my life because I was too impetuous where she was more deliberate and careful. When she finally beat me after thirty games, I got a little... no, a lot worried. I started reading Bobby Fischer and other Chess Master's books. I stayed ahead of her but then she got on the internet at home and figured out how to counter some of the moves I was putting on her and she came back the next day and beat me three out of five.

We switched to backgammon—which she had to teach me—and it evened out because I beat her four out of five times. There was more luck involved with that game. Sometimes we got so absorbed in the games that we lost track of time. Mom would come upstairs and tell Lindsey it was time to go home.

One day at lunch mom told me that I was much more fun to be around now that I had worked things out with

Lindsey. I told her that Lindsey was fun to be around and since I was not exactly football material anymore, I was having fun exercising my mind. She grinned. "Lindsey says you are so competitive she has to go home at night and study."

"Yeah," I said, "She told me she studied chess on the computer just to beat me."

My mom looked at me thoughtfully but just offered me another cookie.

"Mom," I asked, "Why do you think she keeps coming?"

My mom shrugged but I suspected she knew something I did not because she was a girl.

Lindsey turned twelve in August and I turned sixteen. I think we were surprised at how close our birthdays were. We were exactly one week apart. Her birthday was August 12 and mine was the nineteenth. We did not get each other anything, but I made a sign on her birthday and hung it in my room. She gave me a card with a funny message. I kept that card.

Chapter 3

All thoughts of dropping out of school vanished during the summer. When the year started, Lindsey entered seventh grade and I was a sophomore.

In our small, rather rural suburb, all the grades were in the same building, so it seemed natural that Lindsey would ride to school with us. Mom had to take me because the school was not equipped with a bus that could handle a wheelchair.

Lindsey made new friends in school but she always walked beside me when our paths crossed. It became normal for us to eat lunch together. At first, I thought she ate lunch with me because she was a new girl in school and had not made any other friends yet. That was not the case; she quickly became popular. Girls who were attracted to her wit and humor and life began to sit at the table with us. I was behind a year now, so my friends, mostly jocks, clapped me on the back, apologized for not coming over more often and then sat with each other and ignored me or poked fun at me for sitting with seventh grade girls.

There were times when being surrounded by seventh and eighth grade girls was awkward, but that did not last long at all. Boys were starting to notice the girls and soon I was giving advice simply because girls seemed to like me. I had no idea what to tell the boys because I did not know myself. I had no prospects of dating or marriage so I pretty much told them whatever I felt like telling them. Many of the boys asked me about Lindsey because she was new and had a cool accent. Some of the snobby girls turned their backs on Lindsey, but she won their grudging respect within weeks by helping them with homework or complimenting them or befriending them when they seemed sad. In no time at all, I was in the middle of a throng of kids who accepted me as one of them because of Lindsey.

Lindsey was not interested in boys. When the other girls seemed to be falling all over boys, she was friendly but never hinted that she liked one of them extra special. After the boys got used to the idea, things settled down between the sexes. Until they did, I felt like a referee—which was not always a good feeling because it was like being a eunuch in the middle of a harem. Everyone trusted me with secrets, hopes, and fears but no one asked me about mine. I obviously did not have any since I was crippled.

Schoolwork was hard for me. I hated school when I had legs and my skipped year did not make it any easier. I was actually worse off than if I had stayed in school. After a couple of weeks of bringing home terrible grades and falling into a real depression, Lindsey began to take an interest in my studies. She encouraged me, helped me study, learned the subject matter if I did not want to and taught it to me with extraordinary patience. Many a night she would go home at 8:00 p.m., her usual departure, without having done any of her homework. Then she would do her homework before she went to bed. When I was tempted to give up, Lindsey would cheer me on. Finally, she taught me how she studied when she understood my problem: I had no disciplined way of learning.

Lindsey also made me promise that I would not guess about things. If I did not know, I would look it up. She said she learned that from reading biographies of very successful people's lives. Right then we made a pact together that we would stop and write down the topic for later discussion if we did not honestly know enough to argue about it. We talked on almost every topic imaginable. I was amazed at her breadth of interest in things. She was a knowledge hound. At the end of the year, I looked at the list and was amazed at how much ground we had covered. The only topics we did not talk much about were sex, politics and religion. She told me once that of those three, the only one that had facts related to it was sex. The other two required faith while sex required love. Moreover, love was a fact but hard to describe, she explained.

When I caught on to her system, my grades began to soar. Her study method was simple and so effective that I wondered if I should teach some of my former friends who were struggling. All she did was outline the material and then write questions about each idea. We swapped papers with the questions and answers written on them, and quizzed each other. Soon we could ask and answer the questions without looking at our papers—even when some of them ran eight pages back and front! By the second semester of my sophomore year, I began to enjoy the challenge of learning. Lindsey and I would go beyond the lectures, books and handouts. Once we had the questions and answers written out we would research the topic on the internet, going into libraries all across the nation for more detail.

I learned seventh grade material and Lindsey got a head start on tenth grade studies. It was fun.

When I did not have to take finals because my grades were straight A's I teased Lindsey because seventh graders had to take their finals no matter what. Lindsey scored the highest of anyone in her grade. I was not surprised.

Chapter 4

Summer was a blessed relief. I thought for sure I was straining my brain cells and figured they could use a rest.

Lindsey went with her family on vacation to Boston. The second day after they were gone, my dad stood awkwardly in the doorway of my room.

"Hey, dad," I said, looking up from a Louis L'Amour book.

"Uh, I thought we'd go for a ride this morning."

The way he said it made me nervous. "Sure, dad," I said. "I'll be ready in ten minutes."

When I wheeled into the garage to join my dad in the car, both he and mom were standing beside a new car. "You got a new car?" I was surprised.

Mom and dad looked at each other and then grinned. "No. This one is yours."

I sat there in shock as dad handed me a set of keys. "I've carved out a bunch of time this summer to teach you to drive. We decided not to take a family vacation. You don't mind do you?"

"Heck no!" I wheeled to the driver's door and looked in. The Ford was equipped with hand controls. My dad just beamed.

The car was a great thing for me. Just as the wheelchair marked my independence from being completely dependent on others, the car marked my independence from mom and dad chauffeuring me everywhere.

Dad and I spent three whole weeks together while he taught me to drive that car. Since we had fifty acres, there was plenty of room to make mistakes. When he thought I was ready at the end of July, he enrolled me in a Driver's Ed course. The course did not start until September. I wanted to get my license by the time school started but the course lasted three months so the earliest possible date was November. Since dad said he was going to allow me to drive to school when I got my license, I studied hard.

Dad bought the car for me while Lindsey was on vacation with her parents for three weeks in Boston. When she came back, her Boston accent was more pronounced than I'd heard in a long time. I teased her for a few days and then I could not hear the accent anymore. Something else changed about her that it took her going away for me to notice. It worried me. She was...well, prettier.

I watched her walk across the yard the day she came home from vacation. She did not even go into her house first. She just opened the car door, said something to her parents and rushed across the yard until she saw me looking out the window. She waved happily and a few minutes later, she was in my room talking excitedly about the vacation.

Her hair had grown longer and she had impatiently tied it into a ponytail at the back of her head. Her eyes positively sparkled with happiness and it struck me for the first time how much more *interesting* a girl she was. She had grown at least an inch. Something poked out from her chest and for the first time since I'd known her, I realized she had actual breasts and that she was not wearing a bra. She realized I'd lost focus on her words and stopped talking.

"What's the matter?" She asked.

"Nothing..." I hedged. "It's just that your Boston accent is really back!" I said *Bawstahn*.

She grinned and began talking about the things she had seen and done. "I never really went to the Hancock tower or the Boston Common, or anything when we lived there! It's neat. I want you to go sometime."

She leaned over and brushed my cheek with a kiss. "I've gotta go. I promised mom I wouldn't stay very long. She wants me to help her unpack."

I put a hand to my cheek as I watched her walk across the yard. I noticed for the first time that her hips actually swayed when she walked. I had a passing thought that maybe she was walking like that because I was watching. In a way, it made me mad because physical intimacy with girls would be something denied to me for the rest of my life. I turned and wheeled away.

The next day I remembered and told her about my car. She squealed with delight and made me take her down to the garage and show her. She wanted to go for a ride but my dad said I was not ready for passengers yet and that I had to get my license and drive for a while before he would let me take her. That was disappointing but gave me something to anticipate.

That summer Lindsey made me go outside. She wanted to learn archery so my mom talked my dad into setting up targets and a backdrop in the woods behind our house. I found that I could shoot with some accuracy and before long, that was a competition too. Lindsey wasn't strong enough to use the bigger bow so we kept the distance under fifty feet.

Lindsey pretty much spent all her free time in my room hanging out when we were not practicing archery or bird watching. For some reason she really enjoyed doing the things that people in wheelchairs could do.

On Lindsey's thirteenth birthday that summer, I made mom take me to the mall. I wanted to get her something that acknowledged how grown up I thought she was—

especially after saying she was ten when we first met! I found a stone chess set and gave it to her. She loved it. She insisted that we keep it in my room so we could play on it, so that is what we did.

I celebrated my seventeenth birthday and mom invited the Andersons over. It was a nice party. Probably the best part of it was that we played board games as teams and Lindsey and I easily beat our parents.

Afterwards, when the Andersons had gone home, my mom and dad sat talking with me on the back porch. Well, my mom talked while my dad was at least present.

"You two make an awesome team," my mom said. "She's a very bright girl."

My dad lit a cigarette and nodded. He usually did not contribute much to the conversation. Things had gotten a little easier between my dad and me since Lindsey had come on the scene. His eyes lit up when she was around and he had been glad to set up the archery range.

"She's pretty cool. It's like having a kid sister around sometimes, though." I smiled. "She challenges me about stuff that none of my other friends ever did. I cannot just spout off opinions without backing them up. She asks "why" and "how" and "what if" until my head explodes! When she gets excited her Boston accent comes back big time!" I laughed again. "Sometimes I just watch her when she's studying. It is as if she is doing two things at once. She is taking notes and reading at the same time. I never saw anyone as excited about learning as she is.

"I find myself asking why now. Before this year, I really struggled with math. I told Lindsey that I didn't like it and she gave me so much grief about it that I finally said, 'Well, teach me if you're so smart, you little turd.' Oops." I caught the shocked look on my mom's face. "I didn't mean it mean, mom."

"I'm surprised she lets you get away with that!" My mom said.

"Anyway, she did teach me. I actually understand math and geometry. She's studying algebra—which isn't even her subject—so she can tutor me!"

My mom seemed surprised at that.

"I taught her chess and now I'm worried that she's going to beat me every time we play!" I looked at my parents conspiratorially, "I had to ask her to teach me her favorite game, backgammon, just to keep from getting beat in chess. Oh, too late. She did beat me! She goes home at night and looks up stuff on the internet and in her home "library" just to make me feel stupid sometimes. I don't mean she does it to make me feel stupid, but its stuff I should know and when I don't I feel dumb." I was moving the wheel of my chair back and forth. My mom always called it "pacing" and she gave me a look to make me stop. I put my hands in my lap. "She comes over with something new all the time. When does she even have time to learn that stuff?" I gazed at my mom and dad but did not see them.

"I know what I'll do! We haven't talked about poetry yet!" I looked at my parents, "Dad, mom, who's your favorite poet?"

My dad shrugged but my mom seemed to be struggling with some inner tickle. A smile kept playing with the corner of her mouth. Finally, she burst into giggles while my dad and I looked at her in surprise. "I'm sorry," she said, all out of breath. "I was just having a moment." She tried to suppress more giggles.

I'd never seen my mom giggle like that—at least that I could remember. My dad and I were curious. I could see him wanting to ask her what was so funny. I tried to recall the last few words to see if they were funny but I didn't think so. My mom got up and excused herself, "I need a drink of water," she said. I heard her giggles turn into what I thought were tears. I looked at my dad in concern and alarm. He got up and went to the kitchen where mom was. It was a little while before they came back to the porch. They had said something to each other and my dad was smiling. I was the only one left out of the joke or whatever it was.

My mom sat down and patted my arm. "I just got tickled at your description of Lindsey."

I believed her. I began to talk again. I talked with great enthusiasm for almost a half hour until I realized that my parents had not said a word in quite a while. I stopped talking.

They exchanged a glance that I could not quite interpret but I guessed it was about Lindsey and me. Something I said during my monologue had triggered it. I looked at each of them and then decided it was time to let them talk for a while. I could have gone on for a lot longer about Lindsey but something in that glance caused me to feel embarrassed.

Chapter 5

Lindsey entered eighth grade my junior year. She heard about the chess club from a friend and asked me to join with her. We went together and found that you had to be a freshman to join. I started to wheel away from the room but Lindsey said something that made me stop and listen with interest and amusement.

"If I can beat every player, will you let me join?"

I turned my chair around and sat in the doorway to listen. The chess club president was a senior who knew the club was not very good but he did not know the rules very well. He hemmed and hawed until one of the junior members, who thought he was good, pulled out the rulebook. "There's nothing in here about ages or grades. That must be a local rule," he guessed.

The president smiled condescendingly to Lindsey and said, "Sure. But you have to beat all seven of us and we play with timers."

"Fine," Lindsey said. I saw the look on her face and knew that look well. She was extremely competitive! These guys were in for a surprise!

I did not want to throw a game so Lindsey could join the club so I told her to play the members and if she got in, I would join.

I got a little sarcastic with the president and asked, "Do I have to beat everyone in order to join?"

The president looked at me without comprehension. "You're not an eighth grader too, are you?"

Lindsey sat down at one of the tables. Her first opponent, the lowest ranked member of the chess club sat down opposite her. He smiled condescendingly and said, "Let's get this over with."

She beat him in seven moves. The boy was so stunned that he just stared at the board in disbelief. "I want a rematch!" He said. "I could have beaten her!"

The next player in line gave his teammate a derisive look. His meaning was clear. Nevertheless, despite his implication that he would not be as careless, he went down in the same seven moves! Lindsey ran into a little problem with the third and fourth guys — it took her fifteen moves to beat them and then she ran up against two good players.

The president of the club sat down next to me to watch and to find out if he was in big trouble when he played her. "She's good!"

I shrugged. "She's only been playing for a year."

"No way!" He said as Lindsey beat the fifth player in just eight moves and then the sixth player in twenty moves. So far, it only took forty-five minutes for Lindsey to decimate the chess club. The president sat down uneasily across from the eighth grade girl and I could see him sweating before the match started. He lost but she let him stay in the game long enough to keep face. She waited until move twenty-one to pin his king in the corner and declare checkmate. He mopped his brow and said she was on the team.

They had a little ceremony the next meeting and we joined. Lindsey and I were soon teaching the other members of the chess club how to recognize chess moves and soon we had chess "meetings" in my house after school. It was a lot of fun and it was good to have friends around. Most of them were there because Lindsey was but since I was the only one who could beat Lindsey more often than she beat me, they seemed to think I was okay. I did not mind. We had to move our meetings downstairs and finally mom said we could only go until 7:00 p.m. on school nights. That was okay with me because it gave Lindsey and me time to be alone together to study until at least 8:00 p.m. She was talking to her parents about extending the deadline but so far, they said no.

We won our first chess competition. Lindsey, I, and Frank Gillette, a foreign exchange student who joined the chess club that year, easily beat everyone that the Class 2A School had to offer. Then we won our next match and our next one and pretty soon everyone was talking about chess. Lindsey and I had an undefeated record going into our match with the only 3A School on our schedule. It was usually not much of a contest for the 3A boys. They came to the match cocky and sure of victory. In fact, they were undefeated in their division.

I was pleased to see that chess was a bit more exciting at Placerville High than it was at our school. Dozens of spectators were there. I noticed the principal sitting on the front row. He watched with interest as the match progressed. Now and then, the kids would ask him questions about chess moves and he would answer. From what I could tell, he was good at chess. I guessed he might be their chess teacher as well as their principal.

Lindsey and I each won the first match in seven moves. We were as surprised as they were dismayed. Nobody had apparently seen the classic Bobby Fischer, Boris Spatsky matches. Our other team members lost as expected and if Lindsey and I had lost, the match would have been over in the first round. However, because we won, we had to play again until we beat everyone on their team or lost. When Lindsey and I beat the second rank, people began to gather around. When I won my third contest, everyone raced over to see if the eighth grade girl could beat a senior chess champion. She did.

Now the 3A boys were not so cocky. We faced our opponents and I grinned at Lindsey. So far, they had not shown us anything that we had not used against each other during our long summer of playing. Lindsey was nervous. I started with a classic Bobby Fischer opening and my opponent, a big, rawboned farm boy, smiled and countered easily. The game went back and forth and I could not concentrate on Lindsey's game. I heard a roar and looked up to see Lindsey with a grin on her face and the first ranked 3A senior looking stunned. I looked back at my opponent and saw that the color had drained out of his face. If he beat me, he would have to play Lindsey. I thought he was going to throw the game to me just to avoid the risk that Lindsey would beat him but he chewed his lip and made a clever move that made me think he was going after my queen. I decided to draw him in and moved a pawn so he could slip in and put me in check with his queen. He barely even hesitated.

"Check!" He called. "And checkmate on the next move!" He was in very high spirits.

I shook my head in pretend sadness. "I guess you are right about that," I grinned at him. "Checkmate," I said, taking his queen with my knight and putting him in mate at the same time.

After that, we were held in awe by our school and a lot of kids became interested in the game. Lindsey and I began to teach the game to anyone who wanted to learn. They could not believe she was so good. When chess competition season ended however, we dropped back into anonymity.

I got my license right on schedule in November, on the fifteenth and dad let me begin driving to school the next day. I felt comfortable behind the wheel of the big Ford and wished that Lindsey could ride with me. It did not make much sense for her mom to take her now that I could drive. But, my dad squashed that. He wanted me to get a little experience driving by myself first.

I managed to convince my dad that I was a safe driver by the end of November. I begged him to go riding with me to check me out. He made me drive all the way to Nashville and back and then declared that I was a better driver than he was. He gave me permission to drive Lindsey to school and back if her parents agreed.

I talked to her parents the next day. Mrs. Anderson was skeptical but I asked her to take a test ride with me. She could determine the route. She almost declined but Lindsey convinced her that it was a good idea. Therefore, throwing caution to the wind she had me drive to school and back while she rode in the passenger seat. At the end of the trip, she gave permission for Lindsey to ride to school with me.

Coming back from school in December that year, Lindsey impetuously leaned over and kissed me on the cheek. It was the first time since she had come back from vacation that she had kissed me and it was the second time ever. I glanced at her and saw some mysterious inner happiness lighting her face. She was smiling.

"What?" I asked.

"I'm just remembering how we beat the 3A boys!" She had a blissful look on her face. "You made it possible, Jimmy!"

"I did?"

"Yes! You taught me how to play. You challenged me and made me study the stupid game because you kept beating me."

I was not about to take credit where it was not due. "You're just so stubborn that you refuse to be beaten!" I declared. "I remember my mom having to kick you out at night because you just wanted to play one more game to get your honor back!"

She nodded happily. "And don't you forget that I'm stubborn!" She put her head against my shoulder. Her brown hair had grown some and hung down on my chest.

That was a first. We were brother and sister in almost everyway except by happenstance of birth. I liked her better than I would have liked any sister. It was probably because she went home at night and because she was not challenging my position in the family. I thought about putting my arm around her as I drove but since I had to use my hands for driving, it would not exactly work. Then I wondered about that. She was thirteen and I was seventeen. Even if I became the slightest bit interested, the age gap was too great and it would freak both our families out.

Before we got home, she scooted over in the seat and the mood returned to normal. Suddenly I was glad that the specially designed Ford came with bench seats instead of the standard bucket seats.

The rest of the school year passed quickly. Lindsey, I, and various members of the chess club continued to play and study together. However, for most of the week and all of the weekend it was just the two of us. Our parents got so used to us being together they just treated us as if we were their kids, no matter which house we were in. Oh yeah, Lindsey's parents put in handicapped ramps so I could visit. My dad had a sidewalk poured across the yard so I could wheel over to the Andersons. I did not ask them for it, but I guess they got together with Lindsey's folks and decided to do it. They realized that we had formed a bond before I did.

Chapter 6

School was out and Lindsey's parents asked my parents to come on vacation with them. Lindsey and I hoped they would agree and they did. We spent a crazy week at Disney World in Florida, and then went to cabins further up the panhandle that we rented together on the beach near Destin. It was a long section of the beach that was private, which I think was for my sake.

The first day I just rested on the front porch and listened to the breakers crashing. I was glad to get away from the excitement of Disney World. There was so much to do and see that you felt like you had to be on the go all the time. I was ready to relax.

Lindsey tried to talk me into going exploring on the beach with her but I knew it would be impossible to navigate through the sand. The wheelchair wheels would just bog down. My dad solved that problem. That afternoon he rented a battery-powered wheelchair with balloon wheels from a nearby rental place. I really appreciated that and told him I did. He nodded.

"When you are ready to go, just let me know," he said. "I'll help you around the water."

It was a breakthrough of sorts. Lindsey gave me a look full of secret happiness in her eyes. I tried to push it off as no big deal. My dad was a strong guy who didn't know how to deal with a crippled son. It was not something he had ever figured he would have to do. I guess there is no good way to prepare for something like that. It was like my friends at school who stopped coming around because they felt awkward around me. I was not like them anymore and they did not know how to deal with it. Neither did my dad. However, he could not exactly stop coming around. The one breakthrough with the archery range did not really create enough of a change in our relationship to be satisfying. He taught me to drive and that was a great time but he had reverted to silence afterwards.

"It's waterproof but don't get out in the water or you'll get dragged away," he warned.

I tried it out. It was a lot bouncier than my thin-wheeled chair. I did not have to push it either! It had a battery. I raced it up the street to get used to it. Lindsey sat on the porch and watched me as I played. When it got dark, I rolled up the ramp onto the porch and let the screen door close behind me.

The great thing about this vacation with the Andersons was that we did so many things together. My mom and dad and the Andersons seemed to like each other. Lindsey and I had become inseparable. It was special out here because there were no distractions.

The first day was our recovery day and the second day was exploration. Lindsey wore a tee shirt over her pale green, two-piece, bathing suit. She was bare foot, tanned and anxious to go exploring. The families ate breakfast together by mutual agreement at our cabin. It was our turn to do the dishes so we hurried to do them before it got hot outside. Finally, we were ready.

The battery was good for at least three hours, according to the rental place, so when we left the cabin at 9:00 a.m., we decided that wherever we were, we would have to start back by 10:30 a.m. or face running out of juice. We crossed the first large dune that separated the cabins from the beach, traveling on the boardwalk. When it ended, we found ourselves navigating across the thick white sand. The electric wheelchair had no problems. It was almost like driving a dune buggy and I began to enjoy the ups and downs of the sand hills. When the going got too tough, we went closer to the water where the sand was packed and flat. There were a dozen vacant, hurricane-damaged houses set back from the private beach we were on. I felt sorry for the crowds of people packed together on the public beaches about a mile from us.

We found a copse of big, old palm trees, and stopped to rest. Lindsey sat on a fallen tree in the shade and I, who did not need to sit down but did appreciate the shade, watched her. She was sweating and we had only been out for twenty minutes.

"Go for a swim," I suggested. The water was bluegreen and bright. The waves were rather calm. I could see a sand bar change the color of the water a hundred feet off shore.

"That would feel good!" Lindsey stood up and took off her tee shirt. She handed it to me and I followed her to the edge of the water. She walked into the water until it was ankle deep and stopped to feel the sand suck out from under her feet as the waves pulled back from the shore. She laughed with pleasure and described the feeling to me before continuing. It seemed as though she walked forever before she was waist deep in the surf. With a backward glance at me, she turned and dove into an onrushing wave.

I envied her. It was great watching her have fun. She raced back to the shore, splashed water on me, then raced out, and dived into the surf. When she was tired of that, she took her shirt from me and put it back on. We went back to the shade to rest and I noticed that certain parts of her shirt were wet.

We made it back to the cabin before my battery gave up. Dad plugged it in to recharge it while we had lunch. It would need a long recharge during the night but after lunch, it would be okay if we stuck closer to the cabin.

After we ate, I got into my bathing suit and put on lots of sunscreen. Everyone went this time. Lindsey walked beside me as I motored over the boardwalk and onto the thick sand. I drove the wheelchair up to the edge of the water. I was anxious to go into the gulf after having watched Lindsey.

With my dad around, I was not as worried about being stuck so I edged the wheelchair into the water.

Dad strapped a life belt around my stomach, the kind that skiers use, and then he helped me get out of the wheelchair and carried me out to deeper water. When he put me down in the water, I floated. The life belt did a great job of holding me up. I moved my arms and dad let me go. I began to swim. The waves scared me at first because they would come rolling in and if I did not get set up right, they would crash over me! I nearly swallowed half the ocean until I learned to get into the rhythm of the waves.

Lindsey loved having me out of the wheelchair. We could swim together. She had a noodle that she used for flotation so she didn't get tired having to swim all the time just to stay out where I had to be so my feet didn't crash against the gulf bottom.

Lindsey pulled me out into deeper water. We challenged the bigger waves, floating up over them when we could and putting our heads down and trying to swim through them when we could not. The water was so clear that we could see fish darting beneath our legs. We floated for a while and Lindsey pointed to something on the surface of the water a few dozen yards away.

"What's that?"

I peered through salt-stinging eyes. "Looks like a bag."

"Let's go see," Lindsey said.

We paddled in the direction of the bag floating on the water. It was easier for me to put my face down when I swam because it helped my legs get into the right position. I suddenly pulled up. "Lindsey!"

She followed my finger. There were more than a dozen of those "bags." They looked as if someone blew bubbles and dropped them in the water. Only these bubbles were big! "Oh, my," she said.

"I think we should go the other way," I said. "Those might be jelly fish!"

"Is that bad?" She asked.

"It is if they sting you."

Without waiting to see if she believed me, I turned and began to pull toward the shore. Lindsey did not hesitate; she followed me and soon passed me. When she could walk on the bottom, she stopped and waited, jumping with the waves as they came toward her. Our parents saw us coming back fast. My dad came out to see what was going on and I told him about the jellyfish.

"Here, let's get you out of the water," he said.

He loaded me back into the wheelchair and I motored up to where my mom and the Andersons were. Lindsey wrapped herself in a towel and sat down in the shade. We told them what we had seen and Mr. Anderson pulled a pair of binoculars from his bag and peered into the water.

"I think they're right," he said, handing the glasses to my dad.

Dad looked through them for a few seconds and said, "Okay, I guess the beach is closed today."

"Why?" Lindsey asked.

Her step dad leaned back in the sand. "Those look like Medusa Jellyfish," he said. "They won't kill you but if you get under them, those long tentacles that hang down will make you think you're on fire."

Everyone looked at her dad in awe. "How do you know that?" Lindsey asked. She wasn't being impolite, she was curious.

"I got stung by one of them when I was about your age. It's not something you forget!"

Dad pulled a Frisbee out of the bag mom brought. "Want to play catch?" He looked directly at me.

"Yeah, sure." I was not sure I could catch one.

Lindsey popped up and unwrapped from her towel. "Me too!"

Dad waited until I backed up about ten feet before he tossed it. I missed it and had to use the wheelchair to retrieve it. I reached down and got it. I tossed it back and it barely got there. Dad picked it up and tossed it to Lindsey. She tossed it back. After the fifth toss, I was getting frustrated. Finally, I caught one! After that, it was easier and I figured out how to maneuver the wheelchair in such a way that I could throw the Frisbee a long way.

It was fun until the battery died.

Dad pushed me back to the umbrellas where the others were. Mom had a picnic laid out and I got out of the wheelchair and sprawled on a blanket. Lindsey came and sat down beside me. We ate, talked, and listened to the sounds of the beach and surf. It was fun. I fell asleep on the blanket. It was almost evening before we went back to the cabins for supper.

✦✦✦✦✦

The next day we woke up to the sound of crashing surf. The wind was so strong that palm trees were leaning. Dad anxiously dialed up the weather channel and found that it was just a storm, not a hurricane.

After breakfast, we stayed on the porch and talked, watching the clouds gather. When the rain came, it came hard, lasted a couple of hours, and then was gone. In just a few minutes, the beach was sparkling in the sunshine. It turns out that the storm cleared the water of the jellyfish so we were able to go back in.

Every day dad helped me get into the water and then Lindsey took over. She loved to swim. We had such a good time in the water that we hated to come out. I felt like a normal kid while we were there. Back on the beach, Lindsey collected seashells and put them in my lap as we toured the deserted, private sand. We went often to our little oasis of trees to talk and enjoy the cool ocean breezes. I felt at peace.

After supper, we would play board games. A small rivalry developed between us. Lindsey and I won so many games that our parents kept demanding rematches. It was great! After the games were over, our moms and dads sat in the living room and talked while Lindsey and I took over the porch.

"I really like it here," Lindsey said one night while we sat on the porch alone. "No school, no hassles..." she looked over at me. I had my eyes closed because I was trying to remember where Cassiopeia was in the night sky. "...Jimmy?"

I opened my eyes. I remembered. I squinted but could not see it. Then I realized she was talking to me. I looked at her.

"I said I like it here."

"I do too. Can you see Cassiopeia?"

She gave me a look but walked out the screen door and looked into the sky. She knew her stars and constellations as well as I did. We had studied them together using an old Boy Scout handbook from my scouting days. She came back in. "It's too early."

Mom brought two cokes out then and put them in front of us. She smiled at me and went back inside without a word.

"It's so great living on a beach!" She said, continuing where she had left off as if I had not asked about the stars.

"Yeah," I had to agree. I sipped the coke.

"Jimmy..." She flopped down on the porch swing a few feet away and put her feet up on it. It creaked, made a squeak, and then moved back and forth from transferred energy. "...Someday I'd like you to bring me back here. Just the two of us, okay?"

I frowned. I looked at the door of the cabin and saw through the screen that mom and dad and the Andersons were talking in the living room. They would not have heard that comment. Then I looked at her face. "What are you talking about?"

She studied me earnestly. "When we get married," she said. Her face did not break into giggles and laughter.

I was startled. My face must have revealed how amusing I thought she was being because she bridled.

"I'm serious," she warned.

"Married?" I was incredulous. I could not believe she would say such a thing. My voice revealed my amusement and consternation. I did not want to take her seriously because it was so weird. I wheeled to the small, round table and put my coke down. As I did, I saw her face contort and put out my hand to stop a torrent of whatever might be getting ready to erupt. "Wait!" I said. "It's just that you're thirteen and I'm seventeen. It's weird to talk about marriage now, that's all."

She bit her lip. I read the look on her face. She thought I was putting her down because she was too young to know her own mind regarding anything as important as that. But as I watched, her face lightened and she grinned at me. "Just remember I want to come here for our honeymoon."

When I did not continue the conversation, she seemed disappointed. I did not know what else to say. A lot could happen before she was even old enough to get married. Moreover, maybe I would not wait for her to grow up! Yeah, I had prospects out there—dozens of them, all dying to marry a cripple. I looked at her tomboyish figure and tried to calculate the future bumps and curves.

She was looking at me speculatively when I looked up at her face again. I blushed. Her statement about wanting to marry me had knocked me completely off my safe, comfortable, oblivious perch.

Two days after that, another strange thing happened. The cabin had an outside shower so people coming back from swimming in the ocean could get the salt off their clothes. It happened to be outside my bedroom window. The shower was below the level of my window because the ground sloped. If people were taking showers and I looked out my window, I would see the tops of their heads almost six inches below the windowsill, depending on how tall they were. That morning I got up late and Lindsey went to the beach without me. I heard the shower running and wheeled my chair to the window to see if it was Lindsey so we could eat breakfast together. I saw the top of her head, long brown hair hanging to the middle of her back, which was toward me. Her body had tanned nicely with all of its exposure to the sun last week and this week. She was holding something in her hand. I leaned, about to tap on the window to get her attention, when I saw that she was holding her bikini top in her hand. The twin cups dangled from the thin, green straps. My breath caught hard in my throat and I could feel my pulse in my temple as she began to turn to face the water. I ducked back from the window with my heart racing.

The rest of the time, I wondered if she did that deliberately because of what I said to her on the porch, that she was just thirteen. I told myself over and over that she must have just forgotten that my room was above the shower. If she did know, she probably thought I was still asleep. Still, my heart thumped whenever I thought about it.

Chapter 7

With our birthdays being close together, we decided to celebrate during the in-between time. She turned fourteen and I turned eighteen. The age gap would have been insurmountable except that she was smart, kind, and my best friend. I knew without a doubt that she liked me—especially after what she said at the beach house. In many ways, we complimented each other. We actually finished sentences for each other or did not even have to complete them. I knew her and she knew me so well that when we picked out presents neither one of us was surprised. We were both pleased.

Shortly after our birthdays school started. It was my senior year and I was grateful, thankful and excited. I wanted to graduate. I had learned so much about life over the last two years that I no longer felt angry. Life was about choices. I made the choice to be satisfied with my lot in life and that allowed me to move on. I could make of my life whatever I chose instead of remaining locked in a prison of anger and pain.

The best part of school was that Lindsey and I rode together every day. Ever since we took vacation together as families, I felt more protective and possessive of her. I enjoyed picking her up in the morning and again after school. I loved watching her run to the car, excited and happy to be getting back together with me again.

The chess club elected me president without a single dissenting vote. I put everyone on a regime of study and we drew diagrams of chess moves on the board during our meetings. We even invented a few new moves I thought, but later found that they were already part of chess lore. A couple of new kids joined the chess club and we ended up with twelve members. It meant we did not have to play as many games per person. We had the same results in chess club the first part of the school year as we had the year before but three other chess club members also became contenders that year. We beat the 3A boys with five members of our club instead of just the two of us. That resulted in an invitation to a championship match against non-division players.

Lindsey and I played constantly in preparation for the contest. We actually made it to the finals by defeating six opponents without a loss.

The finals were a big deal. People came from all over the country to watch. Both Lindsey and I were nervous as the bell rang to signal the final round. She was in a different class because of her age. I noticed that the Placerville principle was there. A bunch of the chess club members from his school were there too. I rolled over and said, "Hi." They did not seem happy to see us.

Lindsey's match was before mine because she was in a lower division. I sat nervously with my parents in the gallery as Lindsey, her long brown hair hanging over the back of the chair she was sitting on, waited for the bell to ring. She was playing the white pieces and had the first move. Her opponent was reputed to be very good. He was something of a child prodigy in music, playing three instruments flawlessly by age twelve. At age fourteen, he had mastered three languages. However, he had never come up against an opponent as determined and worthy as the girl that now sat across from him.

Lindsey began with Bobby Fischer's classic opening. The kid countered with something I had never seen. Lindsey did not move until the first timer sounded and then she seemed to be nervous and frightened as she moved her pawn tentatively out to meet the unexpected move. The kid smiled and made another move that floored me. I was glad that I was not playing the kid because his moves made no sense to me. I could see the nervousness in Lindsey's body. The kid made his third move and Lindsey sat back. She waited until the buzzer sounded and then leaned forward and moved her knight over to protect against the kid's bishop. I saw that she was playing defensively and that was new. My heart was in my throat as the kid challenged her queen with his bishop and I wanted to scream "no!" when Lindsey captured the boy's bishop and sacrificed her queen. Two moves later I sat back stunned. The loss of her queen did what she wanted it to do. It made the boy forget she had the knight in position to take his rook. It was, forgive the pun, a rookie mistake. She captured the rook and the boy bit his lip. He moved a bishop to cover and she swooped down from the other side with her bishop and hit the clock. "Checkmate," she said softly.

The room exploded with cheers and laughter and shouting. I think I did all three myself! Lindsey stood up and the boy she had just beaten sat stunned. Lindsey earned a $1,000 scholarship and a gold medal. When his friends gathered around him to ask what happened he just said he had gambled and failed. I guessed we would see him again someday.

I won my finals match but it took everything I had. The kid I played was smart and he nearly beat me. We were both sweating. I was determined not to lose because Lindsey had won. I escaped by recalling something that

Lindsey had shown me on the internet once. When I won, my parents, Lindsey's parents, and the whole chess club gave me a standing ovation. I also won a gold medal and a scholarship for $1,000 to the school of my choice.

⟨⊹⟩-⊹-⟨⊹⟩-⊹-⟨⊹⟩

Looking up chess moves on the internet, a few days after the tournament, I accidentally typed in the wrong search word and found myself looking at a web site that specialized in chests. I quickly closed that screen and redid the search but a couple of the images stayed with me even as I studied some complicated moves by some new chess masters. I snuck a peek at Lindsey and caught her glancing quickly away.

"Sorry," I said. "There's so much crap out there if you make one little mistake, they get you." I felt compelled to apologize to her.

She did not comment so I went back to my task. I did find myself glancing at her profile as she did her homework and finally she said, "Stop looking at me like that."

Not knowing if she was mad or not, I pushed my chair back from the table and asked if she wanted a coke. She did. I took the time going down the elevator to the kitchen to think. Why was I looking at her "profile" when it was senseless and could only lead to feelings of anger, depression, and the like? However, at the same time—her profile was *intriguing*. She had changed a lot in the two plus years since she survived meeting the mad-at-the-world fifteen-year-old, me.

How did I feel about Lindsey? I had to ask the question as the elevator doors opened and I wheeled my paraplegic self toward the kitchen. I liked her as a friend because...she was interesting...no, interested. She was interested in the same things I was and she challenged me without regard to my handicap. Now if I started thinking about sex and stuff like that, my handicap would get in the way and I'd make a huge mess of something that was going pretty well now—my...no, our lives. Besides, no matter how grown up she seemed to everyone, including me, she was only fourteen.

My mom was writing out a grocery list at the table when I zoomed past her and grabbed two cokes from the refrigerator. She looked up and smiled as I went by and then returned to her list. "Anything you need?" She asked.

"More cokes," I said but she already had that neatly written on her list. I wanted to ask her about the thing that had just happened upstairs but could not think of how to start that conversation. I also knew the timing was wrong. I decided to put it off until later, if I could get the courage to talk about it.

"I'm going to the store in a few minutes." She looked up as I closed the refrigerator.

"Okay."

I gave Lindsey her coke and rolled over to the window for a break while I sipped mine.

Lindsey sensed my mood change and propped her bare feet up on the bed. She was wearing jeans and a pullover shirt that had short brown sleeves but the shirt itself was white. She was in one of those bantering moods I guess because she popped the top of her coke and then said, "So...did you see anything you liked on that web site?"

"Maybe," I could not decide if I should be embarrassed or not. It was completely innocent, except that I might have stayed for an extra few seconds longer than I should have. I could not really tell if she was upset. The fact that she brought it up meant it was important to her. But why?

She looked serious. "Are you interested in stuff like that?"

"No!" I was not upset with her question. Two friends talking about stuff, right? "I just typed in the wrong thing."

"Sure," she teased.

"No, really; I can't look at crap like that. It just reminds me of how inadequate I am." When I said it, I realized how true it was. That *was* what I thought. I said it without rancor, trying to explain. The only thing I hated about being paralyzed below the waist—and this had only recently started growing inside me—was that I would lose Lindsey's companionship when she found a real boyfriend. Despite what she said to me at the beach that time, I knew *marriage* was out of the question. I knew she had simply been impetuous or worse, was just being kind.

"Inadequate?" She threw the word back at me. "Is that what you are?" She grinned. "I'd have used a different word."

I shot her a look: "Been reading a thesaurus again?"

She giggled. Then she saw that I was struggling a little. "What's bugging you?"

I was constantly amazed at her radar. Denying my feelings did not work with her. That was part of her magic. She alone knew exactly how I felt about everything because she asked and listened. Rarely did she disagree with my feelings. When she did, I could hear myself being stupid or selfish. I had to tell her how I felt because she could outlast me. It was better just to talk about stuff with her or ask her to drop it. She respected that request but denial did not work.

"It just got me to thinking," I admitted. "I'm in my senior year—a year late—but still I will probably graduate..."

"...with highest honors," Lindsey shot back at me, interrupting.

"...anyway, I'll graduate and then we'll go our separate ways. I guess I was thinking of that."

She looked at me with peaked interest. "That makes you sad?"

"Yeah, of course!" I shot back. Her question confused me.

She smiled thoughtfully. "I think about that all the time! You're just now getting around to it?" She giggled, "Maybe you should look at the chests web site more often."

I looked out the window. Mom was backing out of the garage and I watched her turn and head for town.

"Sorry," Lindsey said. Then she crossed her ankles on the bed. "It's just that you never talk about girls or girl friends."

I gave her a disgusted look. "Look at me." I pointed to the area represented by paraplegia. "Who wants a dead guy for a boyfriend?"

"Me."

That was so unexpected I choked on my coke. It represented the third time she had said something like that to me.

Her face registered vulnerability.

"Why?" I barely got the question out.

"We never talk about this subject and I know why," Lindsey said as she folded her hands in her lap and stretched her legs across the open space between the chair and the bed. Her ankles were crossed and she seemed at peace. She did not let me respond but continued, "You're afraid to like someone because you think you will just get hurt."

I stared at her.

"You think a girl couldn't like you as a boyfriend."

I shook my head in denial.

"Oh no you don't!" she said fiercely. "Don't deny it when it's true."

"What? Are you going to tell me what I think now?" I demanded. She was not giving me any space.

"Okay," she shot back, "You tell me why you're afraid."

I wheeled the chair so that my back was to her. I looked out the window. The future was lonely without her but, in some ways, worse with her. I could not meet any woman's expectations or needs. That was the curse of this horrible fate! I could feel the old anger bubbling up inside me, and self-pity with it.

"I hate this damn wheelchair!" I slammed my fist on the arm.

"What are you afraid of?" She asked again. She never let go once she sank her teeth into a question or idea.

I turned to face her. "I said I was inadequate. Just let it go at that."

She shook her head. Her eyes were shiny. "No."

I looked away. "I don't want *them* to get hurt."

"That's not your choice," She countered.

"Yes it is."

"No, it's not. You cannot make people happy or sad. People do it to themselves. You don't make me angry or happy unless I choose to let you." She took a breath and said, "So that means I do it, not you."

I thought about that. "So what does that have to do with...?"

She cut me off. "Everything; it has everything to do with you and me!"

I rolled away from the window. "I don't get it."

"Remember when you were so crass and ugly to me at the first?"

I made a face.

"Yeah, me too," she said. "Anyway, I remember thinking that you didn't like me but I realized it had nothing to do with me. You did not know me so how could you have decided already? You didn't like *yourself*." She waited for me to acknowledge her wisdom but I just looked at her. "And, you've convinced yourself that sex is so important no girl would consider loving you because you can't have...it." She finished lamely and turned an appropriate shade of pink.

I looked away from her. She pressed her point. "That's why when I put my head on your shoulder you don't respond. That is why you ignore me when I tell you that I am going to marry you. That's why when I try to kiss you, you turn your face—it's because *you are* afraid."

I could feel a lump in my throat and I had to take a swallow of coke. The lump was still there.

"It's true, isn't it?"

"Lindsey," I started to tell her that it was too early to have this discussion.

"I've liked you ever since you got over your pity party—or at least most of it. You haven't talked about this part until now. And maybe you don't want to talk about it but before we finish this conversation I'm going to tell you that I love you and I don't care if you can never have sex with me. I am going to marry you Jimmy Turner. Do you hear me?"

"You're supposed to be coy and elusive about this boy-girl stuff, or hasn't anyone told you that?" I responded. I desperately needed time to think of a serious response. I hoped that my humorous response would diffuse the emotion of her declaration.

She gazed at me and then spoke simply. "That's not who I am, Jimmy."

She was right about that. She did not play games. Life was too short for games, she always said. I gave her a long, thoughtful look as I tried to decide how to respond. She deserved an equally honest reply. Too much stuff was banging around in my head; I could not sort things out now that I was trying to be serious.

I liked Lindsey but marriage was a concept I refused to consider. I had nothing to offer a girl unless all she needed was a partner—not a real husband. Thinking of it in terms like that caused me to slough off Lindsey's earlier declarations about marriage when she was thirteen. How could she know? I felt myself getting angry.

"You say that now, Lindsey," I said, "but our wedding night would be just like any other night you've ever had... and the night after that and every night of our marriage after that! You might not think so *then*!"

Lindsey waited until my fists unclenched before she replied. Her response was right to the point. "You don't scare me," she said softly. "But I think I'm scaring you."

It took a while for me to get my emotions under control. But when I did, I grinned at her. "If I start thinking about girls and chests and stuff like that, my head..." I pointed to my shoulders, "...might explode." Then I sobered because she did not laugh. "Lindsey, what *do* you want from me?"

I knew she was older and wiser than I was in everything that was important. She reached out and took my hands in hers. She looked into my eyes and said simply, "Stop being afraid that I'll change my mind because my body is changing or that I don't mean what I say because I'm not capable of having my mind made up yet."

I realized that it was true. I was afraid to like her in that way because she was nowhere near old enough to make firm commitments about the future. No matter what she said, it was still true that her attitudes, opinions, and feelings were going to change in the next few years.

"I didn't know I was afraid of that." I did know it—but not until she said it.

"Well, aren't you?" She was persistent.

I looked away. I did not want to talk about it any longer. The subject was too painful for me. I used to dream of marrying someone as beautiful as Lindsey—but marriage was out of the question now. My mouth said words unconnected to my heart. "Isn't it possible for us to just be friends, Lindsey?"

Her face reacted as if I had slapped her. "We *are* just friends!" She said flatly. "Does that mean you don't find me suitable as a girlfriend?" She was starting to get emotional.

"I never said that!" I was shocked by her sudden outburst. It was not the Lindsey I was used to. My brain told me that she was trying to get me to see something that she saw clearly. But I could not get through my own emotions enough to figure that out. Again my mouth spoke, "Look at what this discussion has done!" I waved my hands at the invisible, churning aura in the room. "We're both upset."

"So as long as I never mention that I like you as more than a friend, everything is fine?" She was not sarcastic; she was hurt. I had never seen her get this emotional. She was the calm one.

"Lindsey!" I could feel frustration like lava in my chest. "You have no idea what you are asking!" In reality, I felt like she was demanding something.

"Yes," she said firmly, "I do." Her eyes burrowed into mine.

The complications of falling in love with her were monumental. For starters, I did not really know if I should love someone when I could not, you know...and she was too young to know the future; I did not even know the future! She was a pony-tailed girl with a love for life and a zest for learning...and she had helped me—but was I in love? "I need time, Lindsey." I stared at my hands trying to sort out the obstacles.

She looked at her watch. "I'll let you know when time's up."

I looked up, worried.

She was grinning. She had made her point.

My defenses collapsed. I looked away from her. "Okay," I said. "I'm going to admit something that scares the hell out of me." I stared at her feet on the bed. "I did feel something when you put your head on my shoulder in the car coming home from school after the chess match. The smell of your hair, the way it seemed so natural for your head to be on my shoulder..." I looked at her eyes so she could see that I really meant what I was saying. "I began to fear the day you would walk out of my life on the arms of another man who wasn't...inadequate. I don't want to disappoint you, Lindsey." My voice choked.

Tears sprang to her eyes and she got up, untangling her wonderful legs, and walked the two steps to where I was. She knelt in front of me and put her head in my lap. "I'm not going anywhere without you," she said. "And, as far as I'm concerned, you could never be inadequate."

All I could do was stroke her hair with one hand and wipe my eyes with the other.

At the halfway point in the school year, Lindsey hosted a party because it was the last year for me and two other Chess Club members as well. Then it was drudgery to the end of the school year.

"All I need to do is show up and take the tests," I complained to Lindsey one afternoon as we were driving home. "School has become so boring."

She took her head off my shoulder long enough to show me she was smiling. "Big change for a jock, isn't it?"

"I liked being dumb and athletic," I told her.

"Yeah, right," she commented.

Our relationship was comfortable since "the talk" as I referred to it between the two of us. She felt better now that I understood where she was in her head and I felt better not having to fight to keep from thinking about it...us.

"Where do you want to live, Jimmy?"

The long straightaway allowed me to take my hand off the wheel and stroke her hair. She lived for the straightaway and so did I. "Maine sounds like a nice place," I said teasingly. She once told me that she hated Maine and I had forgotten why.

She gave me the grin. "Really, where do you want to live?" Lindsey had settled the question of our future together even if I had not. Her question made me glance over at her.

"The better question is where am I going to college?" I corrected her.

"Tennessee U," she said. "They offered you a full scholarship."

I turned into the driveway as Lindsey moved over to her side of the bench seat. It would not do for her parents or mine to suspect romance of any kind. We did not want to upset the applecart.

Stuck to the door was a note from my mom that said supper was in the freezer. I read the rest of the note aloud. *Lindsey's mom says she can stay and fix supper for you tonight. Her dad will be home around 9 p.m.*

"Great!" Lindsey said. She preceded me into the house carrying our books. I wheeled in after her and hit the button to close the garage door. We had no homework, so we had the rest of the afternoon and evening to ourselves.

Lindsey checked the freezer, "Yum!" She said, "Your mom cooked a casserole."

"I've got to do something," I said as I wheeled toward the elevator.

Lindsey was poking around in the refrigerator, looking for dessert. "I'll be up in a minute," she replied.

The elevator door whooshed open. I wheeled in backwards and blocked the door from closing. She normally did not come in the house immediately when we got back from school unless it was to say "hi" to my mom.

"I'm going to be in the bathroom," I said. I thought she needed an explanation so she did not wonder where I was.

"Okay." She resumed her search.

I'm on a regular schedule with the bathroom because if I wait too long...let's just say, I don't exactly know when I have to go and I'm not going to wear a diaper! I went up the elevator and into the bathroom.

It was always a ritual getting personal bodily functions taken care of. It was impossible at first, but dad modified the bathroom to make the task easier.

While I was on the toilet, I began to feel dizzy. I grabbed the support bar. My brain felt fuzzy. I rested my head on the cool ceramic of the sink. The light in the bathroom dimmed. I floated down, down, but never landed.

"Jimmy?" Lindsey's worried voice penetrated the fog. "Are you okay?"

I opened my eyes. The ceramic tile was cold against my face. I had a hard time focusing and my breathing was rapid, shallow. "Lindsey..." I managed to call her name, but it was barely audible. It was enough. The door opened and I saw bare feet and the frayed bottom of Lindsey's blue jeans as she hurried to my side. Then I was floating again.

The tiny green light of a monitor came into focus. I blinked to clear my vision and turned my head. The parts of my body that retained feeling were stiff and sore. I groaned.

Lindsey was reading a book in the easy chair. She sprang up and the book crashed to the floor, but she ignored it and hurried to my side.

"Jimmy!" She said. Her brown eyes filled with relief.

"Hi," I said. My tongue was dry and my mouth tasted awful. Warmth crept into my face as I remembered how she must have found me.

"I was so worried!" She pressed some buttons on her cell phone. "Your mom and dad wanted me to call them when you woke up. They went out for breakfast."

I struggled to get my bearings. "What time is it?"

Lindsey glanced at the clock on the wall. "It's 9:30 a.m."

"Help me sit up," I said. My arms felt weak.

Lindsey rushed to the hall and spoke into the cell phone as she went out the door. In a minute, a nurse followed her back into my room and came over to the bed. She took my pulse and blood pressure. When she was satisfied, she cranked the bed to a sitting position. She watched me until she was sure I would not pass out. She did a few tests, having me follow her finger with my eyes and grip her finger as hard as I could in my fist. She wrote something on the chart and fussed with the beeping monitor beside the bed.

Lindsey moved in as soon as the nurse gave her some room. "When I found you passed out in the bathroom yesterday, I called 911 and they brought you here."

I could only remember Lindsey's feet and jeans. I remembered going into the bathroom and putting my head on the sink because it felt so heavy and full of cotton. There was a tender spot on my forehead. I touched it with my finger.

"Does it hurt?" Lindsey's eyes filled with concern.

"Just a little," I admitted.

Lindsey touched the spot, smoothing it with cool fingertips. "The doctor said you had a clot and it nearly killed you!" Lindsey's face was ashen.

"Was I still dressed?"

Lindsey shook her head no. "Don't worry; I got your pants back on before the medics got there." She blushed delicately.

I bit my lip. My body was so useless! Inside me, tiny bombs could break loose at any random moment and kill me. All this talk about college and our futures seemed like so much wasted breath now.

My mom and dad rushed into the room and hurried to my side. "Jimmy," mom said giving me a kiss, "the doctor says you'll be okay."

"It was a blood clot," my dad said. "The doctor says you need to exercise your legs more often."

"When can I go home?"

They all shrugged.

A doctor with the traditional white frock and stethoscope came into the room. "So, you decided to wake up." He looked at my chart before stepping over to the bed. He put the stethoscope on my chest, took my pulse and did the same two tests that the nurse had done earlier. "Mr. Turner, you are one of the lucky ones. A clot deep inside your leg could have done a lot of damage." He looked over at Lindsey. "Is this your sister?"

"No sir." I said. "She's my neighbor."

He looked at me and then at her. A pregnant silence hung in the room.

"Well, whatever the fortunate circumstance," the doctor said looking at the chart, "if the medic hadn't recognized the symptoms and administered *tenecteplase* instantly, you wouldn't be functioning at all." He watched me while that fact circulated around in my head. When it looked like I got the message he said, "You've been neglecting exercising your legs. We've got to change that or we may see you back in here again."

He went on to explain in some detail that I was at far greater risk of blood clots because I was exercising my upper body but not my lower body. The blot clot came from my legs and stopped my heart just long enough for me to pass out. So many "lucky" things happened including the proximity of the ambulance that I could consider this a miracle. But I'd better not fail to heed the warning. This clot was unusual in that it actually broke up and my heart started itself. In effect, I had had a heart attack with no permanent damage.

"How likely is this to happen again?" I asked.

"Oh, ten to twenty percent," he replied. "Less, if you exercise your legs like you are supposed to." He looked at my parents. "Is he on a regular routine of therapy?"

My parents were pale with worry. "No, we don't have a schedule," my dad said after confirming it with a glance at my mother.

The doctor made a note. "I will set you up with that." He looked at me. "I'm going to put you on an exercise regimen. I want to keep you one more night to make sure that the drugs we have used to get rid of the remaining clots do not cause any side effects. If things look good in the morning, we'll let you go home." He hung my chart up and walked out. In a moment, he returned. "I'm going to have the lab test you for *factor V Leiden* or a *prothrombin mutation*. I don't think we'll find it but I'll know in the morning." I learned later that he was talking about deep vein blood clots.

A short while later, a nurse came in and took blood from my arm. While she was working, my parents, Lindsey and her parents walked out into the hallway to talk. I could hear Lindsey making an argument for something by the tone of her voice but I could not hear the words. Soon they returned and the Andersons said goodbye. Lindsey brushed my cheek with her lips and left with her parents but promised to come back.

"I didn't know about exercise," my mom said. She pulled a chair near the bed and took my hand. "I would have done something, if I knew."

"I know, mom." I squeezed her hand.

"The doctor never told us, or if he did, we were in shock. I wonder why it hasn't come up in our visits to the doctor over the last few years." My mom was searching desperately for a way to ease a fresh rush of guilt.

"Mom, I don't think that doctor took much of an interest in me after the surgery." I remembered the short visits. It seemed like he was always in a hurry when he was in the room with you but had all the time in the world when you were sitting in an empty waiting room.

She was silent. My dad said he was going outside for a smoke.

"Mom, it's not your fault. I do not want you to feel that way. Please."

Tears came to my mom's eyes and she blinked to clear her vision. "You've grown up a lot, Jimmy."

A deep uneasiness was settling inside me, though. I wondered if she would understand if I told her. I did not want her to worry or feel guilty. I decided not to talk about my feelings with her for those reasons. I could feel myself getting angry but not at mom or dad or the doctor. I was getting angry at...God? My body? Fate? I did not know who to be angry at, or with. Why would an invisible enemy that could kill me or cause brain damage in an instant suddenly threaten my life!

My mom could feel my mood changing. "Jimmy, what are you thinking?"

"Nothing, mom; I'm just tired."

"I'll let you rest then." She kissed me and left the room. I almost asked her to stay. Panic clutched at my throat. I did not feel the clot the first time and I would not feel it the next time. One minute from now, I could be dead! I did not call her back, despite the desperation that welled up inside of me. I did not want to close my eyes. I could see the clot forming in my imagination. The silent killer with the power to rob me of what little happiness I possessed made its way up my leg, past my ribs and into my heart where it struck with savage fury. Bitter tears squeezed out and ran down my cheeks.

Two plus years ago, I would have welcomed this silent death. Now I wanted to live! Life had meaning and purpose. I barely recognized the angry, frustrated Jimmy of long ago who sat at the top of the steps thinking about the best way to die. I wanted to live! "Please God! I'm different now,"

I said earnestly. "I'm not that guy at the top of the steps anymore!"

Mom and dad returned. As the afternoon wore on, they tried to carry on a conversation with me but all I could think about was that blood clot working its way up to my heart or brain. I answered in monosyllables. I wanted them to be there but I was feeling intensely sorry for myself. I was imagining myself dead or lying forever in a vegetable ward in the state hospital and mom and dad visiting once a month, hoping I would get better but knowing I wouldn't. When they left to go home at 6:00 p.m. mom asked me if I wanted her to stay.

"No, its okay, mom; I'll be fine," I lied. I kissed them both. I imagined I was kissing them for the last time.

"Lindsey is going to come by later," my mom said. She hoped that I would feel better but that only made me feel worse. I tried to cover it up.

"Okay."

My mom started to say more but decided against it. She and dad left.

I watched the clock tick one second after another until the second-hand completed a full circle. At which one of those dots on the clock would a new clot break free and do its terrible work? When would it sap me of my ability to think, eat, breath, or love?

My gaze constantly moved to the clock on the wall. I hated the clock. It represented that which we all have in common—except some of us have less of it than others. Why did it happen now, just as I was finding a small bit of happiness again? I gritted my teeth so hard I felt my jaw ache. Stop teasing me with this roller-coaster life! Just get it over with! Finish it!

Why is it, that life's playing field is so unevenly portioned out to the players? Why do some of those on the playing field walk from one end to the other without ever seeing a single obstacle, while others, like me, trip over them with every step!

Even more unfair and unkind was that it was not just my life that was being played with so cruelly. It was my mom's and dad's lives too. I had just had the best experience with my dad since the accident. I just made things right with my mom a short time ago and now it was starting all over again. I was cursed to live a life of tragedy.

The clock ticked and ticked and ticked. I wanted to get up and pull the battery out of its body. I wanted the clock to die so I could live! I closed my eyes to get the image out of my head. Nurses woke me up one after the other. Some came to push on my legs, some to check my pulse and temperature, and all of them to remind me that they existed because of the obstacles that abounded on the playing field.

What did life hold for me except uncertainty? I should have said "no" to Lindsey that day. "No, I don't want you to come back!" It would have been kinder than to let her fall in love...my heart clutched in my chest. She was in love with me! Oh, dear God! We were friends but it had become more than that! I had to say "no" to her now, before it was too late. Before the strings became ropes between our hearts. I would be the hermit that fate intended me to be. I would stop resisting it. My mom and dad were involved, we could not change that—it was their fate. They were destined to it. School—that was a joke! Friends were around as long as you could give them something that *they* needed. I could give them nothing.

Jimmy Turner would be a vague memory of tragedy to them, "Remember that boy...what was his name? You know, the kid whose mom hit the tree?"

We are just ticks away from being insignificant to a whole lot of people. My new so-called friends would forget me as easily as my jock friends had forgotten me. The best thing I could do would be to ride the elevator to my bedroom and find my happiness in puzzles and books.

I would be Charlie in *Flowers for Algernon*. It would be my fate to have tasted a better life and to watch it slip from between my fingers *twice*! The only hope that thought offered me was that Charlie was happier with an IQ of seventy than he was as a genius. I knew why too. He no longer worried about other people as if he were responsible for their well-being and happiness. All of those worries melted away with his diminishing IQ and he was able to enjoy the fleeting time he had left.

Perhaps the clot would cause a stroke. Then *I* would not be the one suffering. That selfish thought tugged at my mind like a little boy trying to get his dad's attention. It was a terribly selfish thought.

Which brought me back to the original thought; it would be far better for me to say "goodbye" to Lindsey now, than to wait for the rope to thicken until the clot that took me tore her life apart too.

My heart felt like a lump, a rock, a piece of shriveled up gore that had no more purpose or use in the world than the dead dog rotting on the side of the highway. Nobody cared except the occasional tenderhearted girl who looked out the car window and exclaimed, "Oooh."

"Oooh," I muttered aloud. "That's what they'll say about Jimmy Turner: Died of a blood clot because life was out to get revenge." Revenge for what? My fingers curled into angry fists. How long could I go up and down on this roller coaster? How could life be so great and then so horrible?

The clock kept ticking.

The sun was losing its battle to stay in the sky. Its rays filtered through the Venetian blinds and cast horizontal shadows across the room. I saw it as a picture of my life. I felt vulnerable and afraid for the first time in a long time. I hated that an unseen enemy could be inside me, threatening to break loose any moment to rob me of what little I had left. It just made me angry at…everything.

I needed distraction. I pressed the remote that turned on the television but nothing interested me. I tried to think but I could not. I tried to read but nothing made sense. I closed my eyes to shut out the relentless ticking of the clock.

When I woke up Lindsey was watching me with a half-smile on her face. The clock was ticking over her left shoulder, reminding me that the smile on her face was temporary just like my life.

"What time is it?" I asked.

She glanced at the clock. "It's 10:00 p.m."

"How come they let you stay? I thought visitors had to be sixteen or older?"

"You're feeling better," she said tongue-in-cheek. It was classic Lindsey. Meet fire with humor.

It did not work. I did not want it to work. Lindsey was the one person who would say "Oooh! We have to stop and help the dog." She would be the real victim of this tragedy. I did not want that. She needed to stop wasting her great talent and love on a hopeless cause. Walk away, please! I could not say that aloud. I rolled my eyes.

She scooted her chair closer and put her head on my pillow. "I'm glad you're awake," she said. She was happy to be with me. I bit my lip.

"Jimmy?" Lindsey touched my face.

"I don't want you here," I said flatly. Tears squeezed out of my eyes.

The look on her face was shock that registered in stages. It had been a long time since she heard words like that from my mouth. I watched it register but suppressed the guilt it evoked in me. She was wasting her life on me and it took this demon inside to remind me how vulnerable I really was. If I loved her, I would push her away before it was too late. And I had to do it.

"Why not, Jimmy?" The hurt in her voice pricked my heart. The fact that she lost her humor and there was a touch of fear in her voice hurt more. "I had to beg and plead with my dad and mom to let me stay with you tonight." I was not used to hearing her beg. My heart beat wickedly inside my chest. I nearly relented.

I turned my face toward her fresh, young, beautiful face and said, "I won't have you wasting your life and your pity on me!" I tried to mean it.

"I'm not going away!" She put an arm over my chest. Her eyes flashed, making the green flecks appear phosphorescent. "And if you are having a pity party, it can stop right now!" She burst into tears. "I sat here all night last night waiting for you to wake up! I'm scared to death, Jimmy. Don't you dare tell me you don't want me here! Don't you dare tell me anything but that you're going to do everything the doctor says..." She broke down, unable to express the hopes and fears pent up inside her. She was crying into the pillow on my bed.

A nurse looked into the room and started to come in and say something—probably to boot Lindsey out—but someone said something to her in the hallway and she just turned and walked away.

I waited until she stopped crying. "I don't want to give you half a life," I said earnestly. "I tried to tell you a dozen times but you won't ever listen. I don't have anything for you!"

Lindsey wiped tears with a Kleenex, then got up, and brought the box over to the bed. The nurse had lowered the bed after I fell asleep earlier, so I was horizontal. A triangle dangled above my head, so I could lift myself and adjust position. A catheter dangled by the side of the bed.

"I don't *want* anything from you!" She said blowing her nose loudly.

"Then why can't you leave me alone?" I heard it the same way she did but I meant it to sound like a question. It did not sound at all like a question.

The pain on her face was worse than death. I had wounded her severely. "Do you really want me to leave you alone? Are you telling me that you really don't want me around anymore?" She used those words once before, when she was eleven years old and I had tormented her and told her to go the park instead of coming over to be with a crippled boy. If I would have said go away, what would have happened?

I did not answer because I simply could not continue to hurt her. I was no longer certain that I was right. The hurt on her face told me I was wrong, dead wrong! But it would hurt worse if I did not end it now. Why is it that you can never end a relationship gently? Why does someone have to get hurt? Why do both people have to get hurt? What kind of a world is this when you have to hurt someone to protect them from hurt?

"Do you Jimmy?" She repeated her anguished question.

"Yes." I could not look at her face. My heart told me I was wrong, as wrong as anyone had ever been in the world.

Nobody was this wrong! The word came out of my mouth as if my tongue was not attached to my heart. It just came out. Yes. The most wicked word in the human language. Yes! I want to hurt you. Yes! I want to get rid of you. Yes! I want to dash all your sacrifice, pain, hopes, and fears!

My heart could not believe my tongue had spoken the wrong word. It wanted my tongue to say NO! A thousand times no. Don't go, don't leave. You are the only friend I have in the world. You told me you loved me and now I am saying the most horrible cruel thing I could. Yes, I want you to go. How could I say that?

She stood up, wiped salty tears from her eyes, and then gathered up her things. She gave me one long look and then stepped over to the bed and kissed me on the forehead. When she straightened up, she had to dab her eyes again. Then she walked across the room toward the door.

Everything inside leaped up and shouted at me to call her back. Every step she took with her back to me was as if someone was hammering nails into my chest. It felt like a weight had been dropped on me and I could not breathe. I wanted to beg her to forgive my stupid words.

She stopped at the door and turned. She clutched her possessions in front of her chest and she looked fourteen years old. Her face was pale with tear streaks. Her hair twisted and clumped together from lying on a tear-wet pillow. In slow motion, she lifted her hand, wiped her eyes, and was gone. I heard her steps echo into oblivion in the empty hospital corridor.

Chapter 8

"Jimmy, you fool!" I condemned myself. Bitter, self-pity brought more tears to my eyes. My life was over. I turned my face into the pillow and ground my teeth. I did not care if I shattered them. I would welcome the pain. It would be continuing proof that I was on the wrong side of the obstacle course. My teeth did not break. I bit the pillow as hard as I could bite it. I ground my teeth against the lumps of poly fiber in the pillow. I tasted the dry cotton of the starched pillowcase and hurt as I'd never hurt during the worst moments of my life to this point.

It was for the best. I did not deserve someone like Lindsey anyway. She ought to have a man who could keep up with her intellect and energy and force. She was destined to great things that my wheelchair and blood clots would keep her from achieving...I tried to find comfort in my rationalizations. By now, she was in the lobby downstairs with tears streaming down her cheeks, calling her mom and dad to come get her. I would never see her again except through my binoculars when she walked out of her house on the arms of another man...She would glance across the yard knowing I would be watching from my window, and she would smile sweetly at her boyfriend to show me that I should not worry about her. It was better this way. She would recover.

How I slept, I do not know. When I opened my eyes sometime later, Lindsey was stroking my hair. Her face was tear-stained and her hair disheveled. Her eyes were red but she was smiling.

"You're very hard to get rid of," I said. My voice came out a tortured whisper. I needed something to drink. I pushed myself over, got the water next to my bed, and drank through the straw.

While I drank, she walked to the sink, picked something up, and returned. It was my toothbrush. She put toothpaste on it, handed it to me and said, "Brush."

When I finished, I handed it back to her and she rinsed it at the sink. She came back to the bed, leaned over, and kissed me full on the lips. I responded by trying to turn aside but she took my face and held it firmly and then kissed me again.

I did not pull back.

"Don't ever pull that pity-party on me again," she warned. "I want to be with you—nobody else! I made that choice and it was *my* choice. I'm not going to change my mind because you get scared and lash out." Her eyes bored into mine. Her jaw worked. There was no fighting her resolve. The kiss earlier had steel behind it.

"Lindsey..." My eyes sprang fountains of hot tears that spilled onto my cheeks and pillow. "...will you forgive me?"

The fear left her eyes. She leaned down and kissed me on the lips. "I already forgave you," she said. Then she pulled the chair next to the bed. The clock on the wall clicked and our eyes went to it—11:30 p.m. She put her head on the mattress and put her arm over my stomach. I stroked her arm. The soft skin with nearly transparent hair belied the fierce competitor who, once she loved someone, never quit.

A rush of emotion brought fresh tears to my eyes. I knew I needed her. She was my courage, my strength, my support. The obstacles...well, they had not met Lindsey, had they? I needed this girl...this woman. I depended on her courage—for my courage. I believed in her more than I believed in myself. I would have given up if she had gone away for good. Without her, I would sit in my little upstairs room watching the grass grow in the yard until I died a bitter and angry man.

"What did you do after you left the room?" I asked.

She stroked my face. I felt her breath on my wet cheeks. "I went down to the chapel. I didn't know it was there until I stumbled onto it. I knelt down at the prayer place and I said that I wasn't going to accept what you told me. I stayed there for a long time and then I decided to come back up here and give you a piece of my mind."

"I'm glad you did," I said with a grin.

She put her head down on the wet pillow. "Yuck, Jimmy!" She got up, went to the drawers in the dresser against the wall, and found a spare pillow. She switched the pillows out and then settled her head on the dry one. Her hand found my face and she played with my mouth and nose. When her hand fell slack against my mouth, I kissed it.

"I will marry you some day," I said softly. But she was asleep.

The doctor released me the next afternoon. I was ready to go when the sun came up and so the morning dragged endlessly. My parents came in early and my dad went on to work after he visited for a few minutes. Lindsey went home with her parents at 10:00 a.m. even though she did not want to.

Mom drove me home. She was extremely solicitous, reminding me of the days when she carried an enormous load of guilt. I looked over at her after her fifth look of concern in my direction. "I told Lindsey to go away last night," I admitted to my mom.

She did not respond.

"After I yelled at her to go, she gathered her things and walked to the door. It killed me when she turned her back on me and walked away. I thought I was going to die." The car lurched as mom braked with traffic. She was studying the road so I continued. "When I woke up later, she was standing there, looking at me." I decided not to tell her about the kiss.

"She's tough," mom said.

I shook my head in agreement. Mom meant it in a nice way. She loved Lindsey from the moment Lindsey refused to give up on me that day in my room. "She chewed my head off and told me never to do anything stupid like that again!"

My mom burst out laughing. When she glanced at me though, I saw tears brimming. She looked at the road.

"When I saw her standing by my bed, it was the best feeling in the world, mom."

Again, my mom glanced at me but said nothing. Her eyes still glittered with moisture.

"I don't understand anything, anymore." I looked out the window. "Why is this happening to me?"

"It's not just happening to you," my mom said quietly. "It's happening to all of us who love you."

"That's what scares me the most, mom. I don't want to drag Lindsey and you and dad..." I stopped talking. My mom glanced at me with questions that she did not ask.

"I'm trying to say that I thought about this last night. It's not fair what happened—no, I don't mean it should have been someone else—I'm just saying, I don't want to drag Lindsey down if something else happens."

The car splashed through a puddle. I noticed that everything was wet. It must have rained. She looked at me. "There is this strange fact about life," mom said slowly.

"We don't really know how happy we are until something happens to take that happiness away." She signaled a turn and made it before continuing. "And, it's funny how important the little things are, when the big things are not that good." She shook her head. "I just have to tell you, Jimmy, that you've started to focus on what's really important in life—and you—no, we—rarely did that before. It is as if we did not know what was important..." her words trailed off.

I listened as the tires squished on the wet pavement. The world was upside down. I felt good and bad all at the same time. I chewed my bottom lip. "Last night all I could think about was that I would drag everyone down with me. I would ruin Lindsey's life because instead of liking each other, what if..." I could not complete the sentence aloud. What if we fell in love and something happened to me! I looked at my mom in anguish, "I guess I'm scared that I'm going to ruin Lindsey's life!"

Mom continued to drive, keeping her eyes on the road. A moment later, she reached over and took my hand briefly. "Lindsey saved your life, Jimmy," she said. The doctor said if the ambulance had gotten there even a minute later, the clot might have..." she blinked tears away.

"I know." I needed to lighten the mood a little. "I'm a little embarrassed by the whole thing."

Mom smiled. She touched my hand again. "She's a wonderful girl, Jimmy."

I knew my mom thought the world of her. What I did not know was how she would react if I told her what Lindsey said to me last night. How could I ever tell her about the kiss? That was tearing me apart. Anguished, I looked at her. The confession spilled out, "Mom, she told me she loves me."

I expected her to gasp or something. Instead, mom glanced at me tenderly. "How do you feel about her?"

There it was. Did I love her? I suspected that I did. I looked at my mom's eyes. "When she walked away from me last night, I felt undone. The only thing I had left was bitterness. It was more than a friend leaving. My heart was walking out of that room. I was so relieved when I woke up and she was there!"

Mom did not reply.

"She's fourteen. I'm eighteen. Everyone in the world will see that as weird!"

Mom turned the car into our driveway. I saw Lindsey at her bedroom window and then she was gone. I looked at my mom, "Is it okay if I love her, mom?"

"Is it okay with me and your dad? Or is it the right thing to do?" The garage door was opening in response to the car remote.

"Both, I guess."

"I'm not talking about sex, Jimmy," she said as she put the car in park and turned off the engine. "But love, real love, yes; it is okay." Unshed tears glittered in her eyes as she rested her arms on the steering wheel and looked at me. "You're a different person when Lindsey is around, Jimmy. You are a better person in every way. Your dad and I love her because of the impact she has had on you."

"Thanks mom," I said. I reached over and hugged her neck. Mom kissed my cheek.

Lindsey did not come over until after supper. I wondered why. After the conversation with my mom, I went to my room and thought about my feelings. Somewhere in the middle of that thinking session, I admitted that mom was right. I was a better person now than I had been before the accident. I did not want to throw away what Lindsey had given me and just in case the little bombs floating around in my blood stream took me tomorrow, I knew I had to tell her today how I felt. It seemed as though I had nothing to give her but pain and worry in the future. But, if she wasn't just being stubborn or naïve, then I would give her everything I had until the end. It was true: I loved her.

Lindsey brought dessert. She had napped and then made my favorite dessert out of ice cream, cake and blueberries. She timed her arrival perfectly—so perfectly that I suspected collusion—to coincide with the end of supper. When she walked in the door, my heart flipped with the secret knowledge of my love for her.

The Andersons arrived moments later and sat down at the table to eat dessert with us. My mom *had* arranged it! It was a homecoming celebration and, it turned out that Lindsey did not know, it was also a celebration of her saving my life. Mom and dad opened a bottle of champaign and poured everyone a glass. Lindsey got a little and mom gave me half a glass. Then she stood up.

"Thank God for Jimmy's return home," she said holding the toast in the air. "And thank God for a wonderful girl who knows what to do and saved our Jimmy's life!" Everyone clinked glasses and mom hugged Lindsey and shed a few happy tears. When she stepped back, she leaned down and kissed Lindsey on the cheek. "We love you," she said.

Lindsey's face lit up. To cover her embarrassment and pride she drank the champaign too quickly, burped, and then sneezed. Everyone laughed, including Lindsey.

When the discussion at the table turned to other matters, I invited Lindsey to accompany me to my room. Mom gave me a special look as I rolled past her and I knew she was solidly on my side. I could not remember feeling as good about relationships and myself as I did at that moment. Mom knew I was going to open my heart up to Lindsey and she approved. Lindsey did not know and the anticipation filled me with happiness.

I was silent in the elevator. Mom was right. I never gave a single thought to my relationships before the accident—no, that wasn't true—before Lindsey. She enjoyed life as it came—good and bad, it seemed. Her nearness in the small elevator nearly overwhelmed me. I wanted to pull her onto my lap and press my face against her cheek. The urge stayed with me as the elevator door opened and she stepped away from me. Her scent filled the air. I followed it and her into my room.

Alone with Lindsey in my room, things were so different. I had been alone with her a thousand times, but I never felt this nervous. Love was weird. I should have felt confident, strong, and happy; but I was nervous and sweaty and my hands trembled. I wheeled over to the card table where we first challenged each other and put my elbows on it. I could not think of how to start. Lindsey sat across the table from me and looked at me wondering why I had invited her to my room. I never invited her before. She just assumed that the invitation was always open. Now she sat across from me and seemed as nervous as I felt.

"I should have brought some cokes up," I said trying to cover up my lack of courage.

"I'll go get some," Lindsey offered. She even started to get up.

"No, wait," I said. I reached over and took her hand. She looked so pretty tonight. She had fixed her hair. Instead of the usual ponytail, it hung long and straight just past her shoulder blades. Her blouse was new and her jeans were too. It registered on my conscious mind that she'd dressed up for the occasion. I was happy to note that she had kicked off her shoes and socks the minute she arrived in my room. They sat jumbled together by the door: little white bobby socks on new blue tennis shoes.

She sat back down and looked at me. It was time. I could not put it off any longer. I had called this and had to go through with it. My mouth was dry. "I have a lot to tell you, Lindsey," I said slowly. "Please let me get through it without comment."

"On one condition," she said, her smile tense but bright. "You don't tell me that it's over and you don't sound like you are giving up. Otherwise I'm going to kick and scream and holler until our parents come up to see why you are killing me!"

I grinned at the easy way she lightened the mood and made her point. She also made it possible for me to get started with no more hemming and hawing. She sobered and nodded. I had never seen her so beautiful. Something had changed in her while I was in the hospital. She had grown into a woman. I took a deep breath. "You told me at least three times in the past that you are going to marry me and that you love me." I looked at her for confirmation but she just waited for whatever shoe I was going to drop. She was steady, unblinking as she studied me. The only evidence that she was listening was the sudden narrowing of pupils in those brown eyes. I took another deep breath. Gee! This was hard to say. "I got scared when I woke up in the hospital. I got scared that I would die—that I could die—or worse, be robbed of my ability to think. That is what made me tell you to go away, Lindsey. It wasn't because I don't have feelings for you."

She smiled; a bright quick smile that flitted across her features and softened the worry lines in her face. She had been worried about what I would say! Her whole posture relaxed.

I stumbled on, "The age difference is a problem for me. Nobody would believe that we could like...each other—like that—because we're so far apart in age."

She nodded that she understood completely. I could see the tension lines returning to her face. She began to think that she knew where this was headed. "You always want the truth, Lindsey. I think you're right about that. We can deal with the truth, right?"

She did not nod she just waited.

"So I'm going to tell you exactly what I think, not for your approval—although I desire that above anyone else's—but so that you won't have any false notions about me." I looked at her and she looked back; steady and braced for whatever was coming. "And so you can tell me if I'm stupid." I grinned nervously as I realized I might be presuming way too much about her thoughts.

"It was the hardest thing for me to tell you to go away. It was the worst thing I could have done to you, Lindsey. The worst thing. But you walked away, not just because you were hurt but because you always put everyone else first. After you left I realized that was what you were doing—putting me first. I was wrong, Lindsey. I wanted to shout for you to come back." I looked at my hands; twisted them together. "I was so relieved when I woke up and you were standing there! Until that moment, Lindsey, I thought I just liked you a lot. I'm not as smart as you. I didn't know that I loved you until that moment.

"After you fell asleep, Lindsey, I said something to you that I want you to hear now that you are awake." She gazed at me. Her eyes did not blink but I saw moisture in them as I waited for my heart to stop pounding and my throat to clear. "I said I loved you—and I do."

When I looked into her eyes, they were wet with tears. My cheeks were wet. The Kleenex box was a million miles away. To retrieve it I had to let go of her hands and I could not bear to do that. We both needed it. I finally let go, wheeled over to it, and used the occasion to go around the table. Do you know how awkward it is to hug someone in a wheelchair? It is just easier to hold hands and look into each other's faces. Still, Lindsey did something that was just as good. She leaned over and put her head on my shoulder. Her brown hair fell in front of my chest. I reached as far as I could around her shoulders and rested my head against hers.

She did not lift her head when she spoke. "Do you know why I didn't give up on you?"

"I would really like to know," I responded.

Her hand came up to my hand and her fingers intertwined in mine. "I spent most of my life being afraid of my dad. He was so hard and bitter. He did not know how to treat me. I wondered why he hated me. My mom tried to explain to me why he was like that but I did not understand. It had something to do with how grandpa treated him. My dad drank a lot and mom and I always hid when he got drunk. He never really hurt me on the outside, but I was constantly scared of him. I went to bed in tears too many nights." She took a deep breath. "Finally, when I was eight years old, just after my birthday, my dad heard me crying. He came into my room and sat on my bed. I was so afraid of him that I was shaking. I remember that night because of what my dad did."

Lindsey's fingers tightened around mine. "He wasn't drunk. He took my hand and I was so scared that I grew tense and that is when he broke down and cried. He said to me, 'Lindsey, from the day you were born I wanted to be a good papa. I did not want you to be afraid of me like I was afraid of my papa. But you are, aren't you?' The anguish in his voice was real. I could only nod yes, because it was true. Then he knelt beside the bed and put his arms around me. 'Lindsey, please forgive me,' he said. He was crying so hard! 'I love you more than you could know.'"

Lindsey reached for the Kleenex and dabbed at her eyes. "We talked for a long time that night. He put his arms around me and held me until I knew he really did love me. Something happened that night, Jimmy. I told him how scared I was and he told me how scared he was all the time too. I began to see that he was a real person. I also saw that he loved me.

"But I was still afraid of him and finally one night I told him that he scared me. He sat down again and said, 'Maybe we can have a secret saying that you say to me when you are afraid.' When we finally came up with one, it made us both laugh. Do you want to know it?"

I nodded. I could feel the trembling in her shoulders subsiding. "You won't think it's silly?"

I shook my head.

She smiled, showing teeth that had grown closer together and straighter. Lindsey giggled as she said the phrase, "'O'Reilly's rabid rabbits are raging tonight.'"

I could not help but laugh.

"My dad explained to me that night that he wasn't angry at me or mom and that he was sorry he had taken his anger out on us when all he really wanted to do was love us. He called me his little princess and hugged me." Her fingers tightened again. "Do you know how long I waited for him to call me his little princess? After he left my room that night I laughed and cried because I felt so much better!"

When the silence stretched into minutes, I said, "Did you ever have to use the rabbit statement?"

She nodded. "A few times; but it worked every time! My father kept that promise. He never wanted to hurt mom or me. I even taught mom to say it when daddy was being mean." She looked at me. "I don't think he drank anymore after that night."

I knew when she met me that I was just like her father. I was mad at the world and now I knew how she saw through me so clearly. I was curious about the tears she shed that day I was mean to her.

"What made you cry the first day we met?"

I could see her mind going back to that first day. "You stepped on one of my hurts growing up. My father used to get angry and tell me I was worthless, good for nothing. It really hurt until I realized that he was doing what his dad did to him and he didn't really mean it." She took a breath and smiled at me.

"Ah, Lindsey," I said softly. To myself I thought *I don't deserve you and never could.* I squeezed her hand.

When she went home that night, she stopped at the door to the room, then came back, and put her hands on my knees. She leaned down and kissed me on the lips. "I'm glad you didn't die, Jimmy Turner," she said. Then she was gone.

With that settled finally between us, I found that I actually got much more pleasure out of being around her than I had thought possible. She knew her heart long before I knew mine so it was not much different for her. For me it was like walking into the sunshine from a gray world. Now instead of my world only being in color when she was next to me, it was in color *all* the time. Life was wonderful!

Nothing changed in our physical relationship, except that she would spontaneously get up from whatever she was doing, come over to where I was, lean down, and kiss me. Then she would return to whatever it was she had been doing with a pleased smile on her face. She held my hand and put her head on my shoulder when we were alone...I guess the physical part did change a lot. For me, the best part was that we could talk about love now. There was never any danger that it would get beyond kissing. There was freedom in knowing that too.

The rest of the school year passed quickly. I thought about blood clots but stopped worrying about them.

Most of the seniors had trouble studying after Christmas. I had no trouble at all. Lindsey learned for the sheer pleasure of learning. It was impossible not to feel the same way when she was around. She wanted to learn what I was learning and taught me her subjects too under the pretense that I was helping her.

I graduated with honors because of Lindsey. She pushed me to know more than the books and study sheets. Her thirst for knowledge built a hunger in me too. She was not surprised when the student body asked me to give the Valedictory speech.

I wondered how I could use what I had learned from Lindsey's approach to life. I wanted to thank her publicly—but it would be uncomfortable for her if I spoke her name.

I started cataloging the things that were different since Lindsey stuck her head in the door and invited herself into my life. It seemed impossible to me that she had actually been eleven years old back then. She physically looked eleven years old but her attitude and her uncompromising standards gave her a maturity beyond her gapped teeth and ponytails. I thought about how kind and gentle she had been in all of her dealings with me over the last two years. How many times had I felt like I was the youngest? Sometimes it was just embarrassing!

I thought back to the hospital—what did I learn from that? I learned she refused to give up. She refused to let fear rob her of today. Oh, man! That was it. Lindsey lived in *today* better than anyone I knew. That thought was too heavy, so I pushed it to the back of my mind.

Lindsey never guessed her way through life. She really wanted to know why and how. I could not count how many times she stopped a conversation we were having and wrote the topic down. "We should learn about that," she would say. The next day she would pick up the topic again—having done a ton of research. The girl never watched television. She considered it a waste of time. I found her more fun to be with than the television. The television I could not live without before Lindsey was gathering dust in the corner.

I pondered my speech. I looked at the list of things to research that Lindsey and I had written. I counted forty-eight topics that we had come back to because she said we were just blabbering about stuff we did not understand. Dolphins, constellations, sand, specific algebraic equations...I laughed aloud—amazed at the variety and volume of topics we had researched.

We had laughed a lot. Sometimes I laughed until my stomach hurt and I could barely breathe. It was not because she was trying to be funny, she just was. She had a simple way of disarming the angriest of moments. I suddenly remembered her saying the words "fucking and shit"—the only time I ever heard her say them—and how it completely disarmed me. I tried to remember the last time I cussed. I could not remember. I did not need to cuss anymore. Before the accident, my vocabulary was very limited and full of slang with cuss words sprinkled in to impress my friends who were trying to impress me. All that changed. Lindsey simply said once, *"You don't need to cuss,"* and she was right. Before Lindsey, I cussed all the time in my head because of my anger at being in the wheelchair. I hated that everyone saw my wheelchair before they saw me. Lindsey saw me. She never saw the wheelchair. That was her gift!

I did not know how to express that single idea—Lindsey saw *me* after the accident! She saw *me*, not the wheelchair. She was interested in me, not in how I felt about sitting in a wheelchair or being handicapped. She looked at me and saw something everyone else was having trouble seeing. With her around, I did not need to curse because the anger had simply evaporated like mist dissolved by the sun.

I began to write disjointed ideas and thoughts. I knew I would not use notes—I would not need them when it was time to sit and deliver. When the time came, I knew what I would say.

On graduation day, I donned cap and gown with the extra gold braid reserved for the top ten percent and the tassel that signified valedictorian. I studied my image in the mirror. I had come a long way since the accident. Looking into the mirror, I realized that I liked who I was now. Thank you, Lindsey.

The cafeteria or the gymnasium held the graduation ceremony depending on the number of people expected. This year it was in the gymnasium, not because of an anticipated large crowd, but because the cafeteria stage had no ramp. With only sixty-four students graduating, the school planned for 300 people in addition to the students. It turned out that they had to scramble to get chairs from the cafeteria to handle the overflow. Almost 600 turned out.

The last thing on the agenda before the graduates got their diploma was the valedictorian speech. I knew everyone was anxious to get out of the gymnasium so I kept my speech short. When the principal announced my name, I rolled out of the front row and turned my chair to face my classmates. A microphone was on a stand and the principal handed it to me before he sat down. There was clapping and cheering before I even started speaking so I had to wait a minute for it to die down. That was embarrassing.

I nodded to my fellow graduates. They seemed interested. The bleachers and the chairs at the back of the gym were full. I took a deep breath, hoping I was going to say something worth hearing.

"Classmates, Teachers, honored guests; it is my honor to speak before the graduates of Cross Field High School. Thank you for giving me this opportunity. Three years ago, I was a sophomore practicing on the varsity football team with just the normal worries that affect the majority of us. In only five seconds one afternoon, driving home with my mom, chatting about something I cannot remember, my life changed.

"Some of you look at me and say that it changed for the worse that day. I agreed with that for a year. I think I know what made it so hard. People no longer saw Jimmy Turner, they saw the wheelchair and a poor crippled boy whose life was greatly diminished because he could no longer use his legs to play football, tennis, and soccer...you name it. Even my friends no longer saw me—instead, they saw the wheelchair. And guess what? I saw the wheelchair too. It was the

> *first thing I saw in the morning and the last thing I saw at night. All day long, I saw the wheelchair. I sat for nearly six months looking out the window of my bedroom thinking of all the reasons why I should and did hate my diminished life."*

Babies cried, people coughed, but nobody was walking out yet. I thought that was a good sign. Lindsey was in the bleachers to my right but the glare from the spotlight on the stage kept me from seeing her clearly. I continued.

> *"A year after the accident, just before I came back to school, someone walked into my life...someone who couldn't see my wheelchair. At first, it made me angry that this person did not see my obvious and compelling reason for being mad at the world. This person refused to bow before my anger but instead simply and bravely saw what was deeper, and began to acknowledge that person instead of the one everyone else noticed."*

A murmur went through the audience as people guessed whom I meant.

> *"Since then, I watched that person do the exact same thing for people with invisible handicaps. I say invisible because I have learned of other handicaps that limit me besides the one represented by this wheelchair. I speak now of fear, intimidation, laziness, and feelings of worthlessness. We all share these invisible handicaps. They keep us from doing. I am not going to finish that sentence. A handicap keeps you from doing, period.*
> *"We are not going to be overcome by our handicaps unless we admit and believe that they have defeated us. A handicap may keep us from doing one or two*

things...or even a hundred things...but there are a million possibilities that lie waiting to be picked up all around us. Why should fear or discouragement keep us from doing any of those things?

"Here's what I think the secret to our future success is: admit that you have a handicap and then press on with your life. I think the greatest thing that this person, this friend taught me, is that once I stop focusing on my wheelchair, nobody in this world can use it against me. If I stop focusing on my fear or my anger or my discouragement, I can get on with life

"Seniors, we've got a lot of living left, let's get on with it!"

People were standing and clapping as I rolled back to my place in line. A few were wiping tears from their eyes.

Chapter 9

Lindsey and her parents drove off to Boston for their annual vacation in June, just after school let out. As I watched them disappear down the street, I thought of how much I would have enjoyed another summer at the beach. Lindsey was the same indefatigable girl that she was when she poked her head in my door three years earlier. I could almost mark the day in June that it happened. I was a different person. I tried to sort it out in my head and decided that one day I would have to write a book about Lindsey. I could not shake the twin emotions inside of me. First, that Lindsey was too young for me to miss her the way I was missing her and second, I missed her anyway!

Dad and mom wanted to go to Pennsylvania to see the Civil War battlefields and soak up the history of that period. We left a few days after our neighbors did. The cemeteries were somber reminders of what can happen when a nation disagrees with itself. Rolling through the well-manicured graveyards with cannon and other artillery pieces on display near the headstones, I began to think about what Lindsey said to me—about her desire to be with me for the rest of her life.

She saw everything differently than I did. She saw marriage as companionship whereas I had been looking at it as a physical relationship. The more I tried to sort that out, the more sense it made to me. Lindsey did not see the world in physical terms. It dawned on me that Lindsey did not discriminate the way other people did. She did not strive to be with the "popular" girls. The girl that the boys all made fun of because she was awkward and pudgy and unpopular, Lindsey reached out and pulled into our group. That girl was a lot of fun to be with when she realized that Lindsey, and by extension the rest of us, liked her just as she was. The so-called "popular" girls were welcomed as easily as anyone else was. Hanging around Lindsey, we learned to look for, and enjoy, the person buried underneath the façade of self-consciousness or importance.

I really missed Lindsey.

When we returned exhausted from vacation, mom went with me to Tennessee University for orientation. The campus was huge. I was not the only freshman in a wheelchair; there were a dozen or so. I met a couple of them during the lulls in the speeches and tours. Coming from a small school where I was the only person in a wheelchair, it was a huge change to see handicap parking places, ramps and wide doorways and dozens of wheelchair students. I was going to like this school!

When our birthdays rolled around in August, we had already begun the tradition of celebrating mid-way between them. Four days after Lindsey's birthday and three days before mine, Lindsey took me to dinner. She made me drive to our favorite restaurant and then afterwards, she made me drive to our hill. Our hill was the one place from which you could see the lights of Nashville way off in the distance. We held hands and talked. Lindsey put her head on my shoulder and then, because there was no wheelchair with bulky handlebars in the way, she put her arms around me and I put mine around her. I smelled the strawberry shampoo she had used and the soft scent of baby-powder deodorant but my eyes were looking over her head into the future. What would that be for us? How could there be a future? Then she noticed my distance and brought me back by lifting her lips.

Tennessee University was thirty miles from home and I took them up on their full scholarship. A great benefit of TU was that I could commute. That meant I could be home at night and could take Lindsey to High School in the morning.

I decided on the medical field—not to be a doctor—but to be a medical scientist who specialized in blood disorders. I was interested in how clots formed and what I could do to help handicapped people who were prone to get them. I did not know until later that thousands of people die each year from clots for reasons that sometimes baffle the medical community. The prevailing theory—and one that seemed to be accurate—was that clots resulted from inactivity.

College was a welcome change of pace for me. I loved the campus and it blew me away that the Profs and students ignored my wheelchair. We were there to learn and it was refreshing to know that I was lumped right in with ambulatory students because the school was interested first in training student's minds. I attended classes and went home to study. Campus dorm life and extra-curricular activities did not interest me at all.

Lindsey entered her sophomore year and immediately assumed the presidency of the chess club--by unanimous acclaim. She asked me to be the club's mentor and coach as allowed by the club rules and I happily accepted.

Lindsey had the chess club organized so that members were required to play at least two games a week against me. With ten members in the club, I was playing twenty games of chess. Much of that happened on weekends so Lindsey and I could study together weeknights. I looked forward to the time alone with Lindsey. We shared an intimacy that went beyond the physical.

My dad supported our studies behind the scenes by bringing in contractors to knock out a bedroom wall, which doubled the size of my room. Mom found chess tables, with built in boards, and bought them. Dad put them in the enlarged section of my room. Lindsey asked her dad to build shelves in my room to hold the overflow of books that we used as reference materials. Then he found a wireless internet service provider and bought two computers equipped with wireless technology and set those up in my room. As if that was not enough, he hooked up a satellite dish and we were able to dial in educational programming. He even put a small refrigerator in my room so that we could have cold drinks and snacks available to the chess club. Mom baked cookies all the time and the chess club began to call her mom.

Sometime in December, Lindsey finally reduced the number of games that I had to play with each of them to one as they progressed in their skills and the games took longer to play. She required chess club members to keep their grades up above a B average—which was not a chore for most of them. The ones that struggled got all the help they needed from Lindsey or me during the week. It was not long before more kids got interested and the chess club started to grow again. Nerds are just as hungry for friends as jocks, and my house was the gathering place. Others were there too: kids that did not fit into any other group fit ours perfectly.

It did not take long for Lindsey to crack down on the kids who were coming for the wrong reasons. She was not mean or harsh in anyway. She simply explained that if they wanted to be part of the chess club they would achieve the required grade point average by getting better study habits or tutoring as needed. (We even enlisted my mom to help with math tutoring and she loved it.)

Lindsey easily handled older kids. She reminded all of the chess club members of the goal they were trying to reach at every official club meeting. *"We simply want to become what we can be by doing what we should do."* It was her motto and soon became the motto of most of the kids that hung around with her.

One night I asked her about the motto. "Where did that come from?"

She looked at me for a long moment before answering me. "I think it sums up what you stand for," she said.

"Me?" I was perplexed. "It describes you far better than it describes me."

She just smiled.

I could not figure out what she meant by that and she was not going to explain.

I knew she meant what she said; she never lied or embellished the truth. She did not have to. The more I pondered the motto, the more I saw Lindsey's life reflected. She studied for the sheer joy of learning. She reached out to others in order to know them more deeply. She was becoming better daily because she kept her footing and balance. I could not see how that described me at all until after Lindsey stepped into my life. It might be true of me now. Perhaps she could not see what effect she had on others. Perhaps she attributed that motto to me because she did not see her reflection when she looked at the mirror she knew as Jimmy Turner. It was true that she learned things from me but that was different. She caused everyone around her to want to live up to his or her potential. She, more than me, lived the motto.

I admired something else in Lindsey's character. She took the hurt for a foolish decision if it belonged to her. She told me once that she would rather take the heat and get it over with than live in the dread of it. I think she was twelve when she told me that. I never forgot it. I watched her apply that principle.

Once, Lindsey broke a dish while she was cooking something for me during one of mom and dad's mini-vacations. She swept it up and put it in a brown paper bag. I urged her to throw it out, telling her that nobody would miss it. It was not that important. I used a dozen arguments that were sound and reasonable, but flawed from her perspective. She sat down at the table and looked at me as if I was a child. "Jimmy, I love your mom. It was an accident and I want her to know about it. This is a little thing but I'm going to keep things clean between us because your mom trusts me with a much bigger thing."

I shook my head. "What are you talking about?"

She gave me a look that made me check to see if I had spinach hanging from my teeth. "Look around you," she said softly.

I looked around me. The clock ticked its way to 7:30 p.m., the kitchen smelled of spaghetti and meatballs, the dishes were done and put away. I felt like I was missing something important. "What?"

"Don't you see me, Jimmy?" She asked.

"Of course I see you!" I was getting upset.

She gave me the raised eyebrow look. I went through the search in my mind again. Nope, I did not see what she was getting at.

"Your mom and dad are gone, Jimmy. They let me come over here because your mom trusts me."

I probably turned three shades of red. I actually thought it was because mom and dad knew nothing could happen between us! Lindsey saw it much differently. She saw it as a trust issue. To my discredit, I shook my head as if I thought she was being silly.

I found tons of information on blood clots and by the end of my first year in college, I felt overwhelmed by the amount of information I had to process. One thing became a certainty from the research; it was vital that I become more active. It was good that I was developing upper body strength but I still had to exercise my legs. As long as blood flowed and muscles existed, exercise was needed. I also discovered that I needed exercise in order to keep bone density.

My dad found some equipment that would help and set it up in the remaining upstairs bedroom. Part of my daily regime was to spend thirty minutes on the exercise equipment in the spare bedroom. Lindsey immediately subscribed to that as well. She had to help me get onto some of the equipment so she just stayed and began to work out with me. For some reason my dad bought a stationary bike—which we discovered I could not manage, but he left it because Lindsey used it.

My first year in college passed quickly. I thought the classes were easy but then I knew how to study, thanks to Lindsey.

According to chess club members who slipped me information about high school affairs quite unwittingly, Lindsey was very popular. The rumor was that she was going with a college boy and some of the girls who did not like Lindsey because she was their opposite in so many ways, began to spread vicious rumors about her sexual desires. The chess club members stood up for her but they were the nerds in school and their voices did not much matter. Thankfully, the antagonists were in the minority.

Some of the teachers did not like Lindsey either. They could not fault her study skills or her test skills but they began to call her a know-it-all and some of them even smirked when she raised her hand to answer questions. Some chess club members considered going to the administration because these teachers were so blatant about not calling on Lindsey and ignoring her responses or using nonverbal language to show their distain.

When I asked Lindsey how school was going, she always told me that she was enjoying it. I asked her how she could ignore the rumors, gossip, and teachers who were being so mean. We were working out when I asked her about it. She was riding the stationary bike and the turning wheel was humming while she considered her answer. "It hurts," she admitted at last. "But they're wrong. If I let it affect me, then they're right." She lifted her shoulders.

"Aren't you going to do anything about it?"

She let the bicycle come to a stop. "I think I am going to do something about it but not right now." She wiped her face with a towel and dropped the towel on the bench next to her. Her cheeks were flush with exertion.

"What are you going to do?"

"I don't know, Jimmy." She looked away and then back at me. "I guess I'll wait for an opportunity to do something nice for one or more of them, if it comes up. Maybe they'll change their minds."

"Do something nice? You can't fight this by doing something nice! They don't like you. They won't let you do something nice for them. They'll make it out to be something bad or say you are interfering or some such crap."

"You don't know that."

I would have argued with her because I was feeling angry towards those stupid people who could not see that Lindsey was honorable, kind, sweet and...and she was right. Because she was not like them, she was going to overcome their handicap in the same way she overcame mine. I sighed. "You're right. I'm just spouting off because I want to protect you. It makes me angry, that's all."

Lindsey smiled at me. I loved that smile! "I'll be okay, Jimmy. Thank you for feeling like that."

I returned to my exercises frustrated with small-minded people. One of the machines exercised my legs and as it did, I wondered if there was something I could do to help the situation—and not make it worse. It dawned on me that Lindsey had taken the same approach with me when we first met.

Lindsey was not soft in the sense that anyone could push her around. She had a mental and emotional toughness that went miles beyond mine. When I thought about it, she simply told the truth even if it she was at fault. That took toughness. She confronted people in such a way that they appreciated it. I longed to have that skill when I needed it. I was more like the bull in the china shop breaking things that did not need to be broken just because I usually had to be mad in order to confront injustice.

The new routine made the year pass quickly. The spring semester gave me a change of classes and topics but the routine stayed the same. I shut my ears to the chess club gossip about Lindsey and boys and teachers just because it served no purpose for me to hear it. I could not do anything about it until Lindsey asked for my help. If she did not ask, she would most likely take care of it very well on her own.

Lindsey entered her junior year in high school as I began my second year at the University. I loved my studies but so far, I had only done the basics. This year I was going to begin studying the science of the body and I was looking forward to it. Lindsey was a straight "A" student and we met every night to compare notes, exchange occasional saliva and do our homework. Lindsey was still in the chess club and on weekends, after homework was done to her satisfaction, we played chess or backgammon.

One evening, watching her as she concentrated on the chessboard I was struck by her looks. From a homely pre-teen with gaps in her teeth, Lindsey had blossomed. She saw me staring at her after she moved. "Like what you see, Mister?"

"Very, very much," I replied honestly.

"Ah, you say that..." Then she giggled.

"My parents tell me that you are bombarded with invitations to the prom."

"Yes, that's true. Every member of the chess club has asked me at least twice." She gave me a coy look. "But I'm holding out for a past president of that prestigious club."

"I would love to take you to the prom. Will you go with me?"

"I don't know. Can you dance?"

I backed my wheelchair away from the card table and did a series of wheelies and maneuvers. "Good enough?"

"I don't think I've ever seen those steps before," she teased me. "How can I learn them in time?"

"Hop on," I grinned.

It was a little harder with Lindsey on my lap but the dance was nice. When my arms refused to work any longer,

Lindsey kissed me and stood up. "I would be delighted to go with you. We'll be the talk of the prom."

There was another reason for going to the prom. I had missed prom both my junior and senior years because I could not take Lindsey. She was just too young when I was eligible to go. I wanted to make it up to her. And, the boys at school considered Lindsey "hot" but could never figure out why she refused to give them a second glance. Now they would know. I thought it would take some of the pressure off her. She thought so too.

I spent an hour on the internet going through hundreds of flower shops to find the right corsage for Lindsey. I wanted this corsage to do what I could not. I could not dance with her physically but she would feel me next to her heart and the rest of the girls at the prom would envy her because her man considered her his perfect flower. I finally found it—a Cataleya Orchid. This particular strain only grew in Hawaii and then in rare locations where volcanic rock and perfect humidity allowed it to bloom. Its texture, shape, and color fascinated me. It was perfect! It was a rare bloom for a precious flower.

We discussed prom etiquette one afternoon. I told her that I wanted to do everything a normal date would. I would get out of my car, roll up to her front door and ring the bell. I wanted to come inside, pin the corsage on her in front of her parents, and then open the door to the car for her. She gave me a look that said it was not necessary but her eyes shone with just the right amount of mist that I knew she loved the idea.

The Andersons were waiting with cameras in hand when I went through the process of picking Lindsey up. My mom and dad were there with cameras too.

The school cafeteria was the only room large enough for the prom. The band was a local group and the kids were dressed in suits or, if they could afford it, tuxedos. I wheeled in as Lindsey walked next to me. I did not know these kids very well. The only ones I knew were the members of the chess club because they met regularly at my house. I greeted a couple of them while Lindsey and some of the other girls went to the powder room to make sure gowns, corsages and hair were perfect.

"Hey, Jimmy!"

I looked up. It was Chuck Singleton, a member of the chess club. "Hey Chuck," I said. We did not shake hands; we did something that resembled slapping meat, cheese and then mayo on bread—a real nerd handshake. He sat down at the table and introduced Cindy Hall to me.

"Where's Lindsey?"

"I think she went to the bathroom."

A few other couples drifted past our table. One of them, a boy who looked distinctly uncomfortable in a suit, gave me a malevolent look. I was not sure if he was reacting to my wheelchair or my age. I looked over at Chuck who saw it. "That's Frank Thornton," he said. "He's got a thing for Lindsey, I think. Anyway, he bugs her all the time." He motioned with his hand, "Those are his two best friends with him."

"Where's his date?" I asked.

"See that skinny black-haired girl sitting at that table over there? That's her; Marci something."

"What do you mean he's 'got a thing' for Lindsey?"

"He's a nut case. I don't know why Marci hangs with him." Chuck's mouth curled in an expression of distaste. "She must be hard up."

I looked around the room. Candles seemed to be the only lighting. Frank and his two friends were staring in our direction. Already junior boys were showing off by holding their fingers over the flame until it hurt. The girls were giggling at their date's antics. Frank was ignoring his date.

Lindsey arrived at the table then, looking fresh and beautiful, and sat down.

The band started playing, Lindsey looked at me, touched her corsage and got up with Cindy, and they danced. It was a fast dance and Cindy already knew Chuck did not know how and Lindsey knew I could not. I watched Lindsey. She wore a long blue dress that made her eyes glow and set off her figure in amazing ways. She told me it was her parent's gift to her. They saved money for it by not going out to lunch for three months! She called it an Allen Schwartz Charmeuse gown. All I know is that it showed off her slim figure magnificently. The gown's hem was cut higher in the front than in the back. I guess that was to show off the shoes. Watching her dance, I decided her shoes were part of the package too. They were single strap, open toe low heels that matched her dress perfectly. I thought she was the prettiest girl on the floor and so did a group of boys who stood and gaped and got scowls from their dates.

When Lindsey came back flushed and happy she leaned down and kissed my cheek. "I was dancing with you," she said.

Chess club members came by the table at various times with drinks and nuts and other items from the serving table. Lindsey danced with anyone who asked—by mutual agreement. Each time she left to dance, she touched her corsage and when she came back to the table, she would sit and hold my hand so everyone could see she was with me.

The band took their break midway through the prom and Lindsey asked me to walk her to her locker so she could get something. I suspected she just wanted to get away from the crowd for a few minutes. We entered the hallway and took a left along the first corridor and then a right at the intersecting hallway. Her locker was at the far end of the building.

When we were alone, she leaned down and kissed me. "Thank you for taking me to the prom," she said.

I patted my lap. She looked at me, concerned that she might wrinkle my tuxedo but I did not care about that. She put her hands on the armrests and lowered herself to my lap. She had to put her feet on mine. She adjusted her dress and I wheeled her down the long corridor loving the feeling of her against my chest and the smell of her hair. At her locker, I held her for a little while. It was difficult to kiss but we managed to do it twice before I heard the sound of feet in the corridor behind us. Lindsey bolted out of the chair and guiltily twisted the dial of her locker as three boys came around the corner. I could hear her suppressing giggles.

"There they are!" One of the boys said.

Lindsey turned. She did not need to speak; her expression conveyed her dismay.

From that expression, I guessed this was not going to be pleasant. I turned my wheelchair to face the boys who were staggering slightly. I figured they had just come out of the boy's bathroom up the hallway.

"What's up, Lindsey?" One of the boys said. He stopped a few feet away from us and the other two bunched up around him.

"Nothing's up, Harold." Lindsey stepped away from the locker and stood beside me. I could feel the tension in her

body even though we were not touching. "Hello Mark...
Frank." She named them all so I would know their names.

"So this is why you dance with girls." Mark, the boy
with a perpetual sneer, said. Lindsey did not react to the
insult. She remained calm. Her fingers rested lightly on
my shoulders as she stood behind me. Mark laughed. "You
prefer cripples in wheelchairs to..."

"There's no need for that," I warned. "Why don't you
boys just go back to your party?" I used the word boys
deliberately and did not think better of it until after I said
it. The old anger in me was taking over.

They looked down at me and then ignored me. They
spoke to Lindsey. "Come on, Lindsey, we'll show you how
to have a better time than you could ever have with a
cripple."

They moved closer as a pack. I smelled alcohol. The
school had certainly changed. I tensed, readying myself
for what might come from these idiots. If one of them got
close enough for me to grab I could do something. I looked
back. Lindsey was behind me and to my left so they would
have to move me out of the way to get to her.

"How is Marci, Frank?" Lindsey asked gently. She looked
at the other boy who was hanging back just slightly.

The others sniggered at this. They knew Lindsey was
mentioning Marci in order to remind Frank that he already
had a date and she was probably missing him. Frank stepped
closer.

His reaction made me bridle. "Get out of here before
one of you gets hurt," I said with as much menace in my
voice as I could muster. The old anger was coming up in me
and it felt good. Lindsey's hand was on my shoulder and I
felt her fingers dig into me. She wanted me to soften my
tone, but I could not find soft words.

The boys stopped moving toward us. Their courage temporarily interrupted by the tone of my voice. "What are you going do, ram into us with your wheelchair?" Harold's mocking voice made me turn toward him. He backed away at my sudden move.

I needed to diffuse the situation and protect Lindsey if I could. I stuck my hand out in a gesture of friendship. "Hey, let's be friends," I said softly.

The move caught them off guard. They needed time to adjust.

"I don't want any trouble, guys," I said. "We're all here to have fun, right?"

I could feel Lindsey's fingers kneading my shoulder. She hoped I would follow her lead. But I remembered Chuck telling me Frank had made moves on Lindsey. I could tell he was upset that Lindsey was with me instead of him.

"Let's leave the little cripple boy and his slut girlfriend," Frank said with the same sneer in his words.

I lost it. I stared at the boy, trying to back him down with my anger. He stared back. When I spoke, it was with calm fury. "You're a jackass." I said it because part of me wanted payback for insults just like that one that Lindsey had endured from stupid idiots like Frank. She was the girl who had changed my life and I was not going to let Frank get away with calling her anything.

Lindsey desperately tried to communicate reason with her fingers but I was beyond reason. Emotion had earned its rightful place and I let it have the reigns.

Frank's face went blank and then, as the insult registered, he bridled and reached for the arm of my wheelchair. He intended to upend it and spill me onto the floor. I reached out and caught his arm. Frank was strong but years of using my arms for everything gave me a lot of upper body strength. My grip was like iron on his wrist. He tried to break free but he could not. The other two boys hung back, not sure what to do.

"Let go!" Frank growled. He was off balance and could not swing at me with his other arm because he would have to swing across his body. I twisted his wrist so he could not turn toward me. He started to turn the other way, to swing a backhand at me, so I grabbed the wheel of my chair with my left hand to act as a brake and then I bunched the muscles and the fury that was building up inside me and pulled him into me before giving him a tremendous shove. He stumbled backwards and lost his balance. He crashed to the floor and stopped after his head hit a locker with a bang.

The other two looked at Frank and then at Lindsey and me. They were trying to decide. Lindsey was on my left side, the boys were on my right side and our backs were to the lockers. They did not expect a cripple to put up a fight. They could come around to the left side and make it difficult or they could just come toward me swinging. As long as they were uncertain, that worked to our benefit.

Frank struggled to his feet. He rubbed his buttocks, the first part of his body to hit the floor, and then his head. "I'm going to make you pay for that!" He glared at me as if that would do it. When I did not respond he turned as if to walk away and then suddenly whirled and gave my wheelchair a hard shove. The other two boys started to come toward me.

I heard a gasp behind me but I could not afford to turn and look. I reached for one kid's arm to keep him from tipping my wheelchair when I heard a shout.

"Hey! Lindsey, Jimmy!" It was Chuck at the end of the corridor. Cindy was on his arm. They had come looking for us. "What's going on?" They began to run toward us.

I was never as glad to see a chess nerd as I was then.

The boys glanced back and decided to leave. Chuck and Cindy moved to let them go past and then hurried to where we were. "Lindsey, are you okay?" Cindy knelt beside the prone form of the girl I had been trying to protect.

"I think the handlebar knocked the wind out of me," she gasped. Her face contorted in pain.

Cindy helped Lindsey get to her feet but she doubled over in pain. "It hurts."

Cindy said, "Just stay there, I'll go get some help."

I wished I could get out of my wheelchair and do something...anything, but I was helpless. She gave me a brave look but pain contorted the gentle features of her face. It took an agonizing five minutes for one of the chaperones to come and listen to what had happened. They tried to get Lindsey to her feet but again she doubled over in pain.

"Call 911," the chaperone said.

A flurry of activity followed. Lindsey went by ambulance to the hospital and I followed in my car. I called her parents and mine from the school. They met us at the hospital and we waited anxiously for word from the doctor about Lindsey's condition. At last, Lindsey's mom and dad talked to the doctor. A little while later, they came out.

"Her spleen was damaged by the force of the handlebar," Lindsey's mom told my mom and dad while I listened in miserable silence. "It would have been just a bruise if she hadn't been pinned against the lockers." She looked at me and then away. "I'm not sure what that means to her health. They're trying to decide if they should remove her spleen."

"She should be okay without a spleen," I said, "They can't repair it because it's too soft and spongy. I just studied about it in school."

My mom looked at me. "What does the spleen do?"

"It's like a sponge that filters the blood only not like the kidneys," I told her. "It removes old tired red blood cells." It did more than that but I did not want to alarm her parents. She would be okay without it that much was true I was almost certain of that.

My mom hugged Lindsey's mom and my dad stood awkwardly beside me. Nobody asked me if I was okay but even if asked, I would have said yes. The only thing that hurt was inside me. I could not protect Lindsey sitting in a wheelchair and I had even been responsible for her injury. If I'd just tried to talk Frank out of his drunken actions instead of manhandling him!

I told my story repeatedly to every official who asked. The worst reaction was the reaction of the Andersons who believed that I provoked the incident. I was the oldest; I should not have used physical force and so forth. I could see disapproval in Mrs. Anderson's eyes when she looked at me.

It was the next day before Lindsey could have visitors. When her parents finally let me in to see her, she gave me a wan smile. "Sorry," she said. "I had to beg and beg my mom and dad to let you in. I threatened to get worse if they didn't let you!" She grinned as she took my hand.

"I'm so sorry, Lindsey," I said. "I shouldn't have pushed Frank down."

"You did what you had to do and I'm proud of you!"

I stayed with her as long as I could but finally her mom sent her dad in to say that Lindsey needed her rest. I rolled past them in the waiting room, got in my car, and drove home. Something had definitely changed in the Anderson's attitude toward me. I could not blame them. From their perspective, once again the boy next door was responsible for their daughter being hurt.

Lindsey came home the next day. I watched from my window as she walked slowly into the house next door. As soon as I could get downstairs, I made my way over there.

I could tell they did not want me there. I felt panic but I did not want to beg. I started to turn around but Lindsey called my name. "Jimmy! Wait! Don't go."

Her dad's lips tightened slightly but he opened the door for me to come in. I waited in the front room. Lindsey wore a bathrobe and her hair was a mess but to me she looked radiant. Just her smile was all I needed to assure me that she did not bear the same grudge as her parents.

She sat down on the sofa and shooed her parents out of the room. They went begrudgingly. What was I going to do, start a fight with their daughter? Geez!

"I'll be okay, Jimmy," she said. "I have to stay in bed for a few days so the sutures can do what they have to do. They'll disappear after a week so I don't have to get them taken out." With the good news delivered, she looked around the room. Her parents were gone. "But there's more."

I caught my breath.

She took my hand. "Remember I told you about my dad?" I nodded. "Well, I didn't tell you what he died from. He had Meckler's Disease. It is a rare blood condition. Only a few people have it. He was one of them. It's genetic."

I kept looking at her. My heart told me that there was more.

"I have it, Jimmy." Tears came to her eyes. She was trying to be brave. "My parents don't know that I know. While I was in the hospital one of the blood tests came back positive for it. My mom and dad probably know because it was on my chart. I read my chart, Jimmy!"

"What does that mean?" I asked. My eyes clouded.

"My dad lived to be forty-two," she said. "I have to do more research on it." She looked at me. "Jimmy, something I was going to show you at my locker! They are doing spinal restoration in South America now but it is an American doctor and his team that are doing it. They have a fifty percent success rate!"

How typical. Lindsey never worried about herself.

"You have to read it!" She gave me the web site name. "Go research it, Jimmy!"

I promised I would. We held hands and talked quietly for a while and then her parents came back into the room. The tension grew so I excused myself and headed for home after extracting a promise that I could visit again after school the next day.

My visits seemed less welcome to the Andersons, but not Lindsey. She watched from her window until she saw me coming and she always met me at the door. She was getting stronger now and soon would be able to go back to school. I missed our time together in my room. I was afraid that her parents would deny us that when Lindsey fully recovered. I wished I could speak to them about what happened but they did not seem inclined to talk about it. How different from Lindsey! They continued, instead, to give me looks that I interpreted as wishing Lindsey had never met me.

I asked my parents to intervene but since I had nothing specific to tell them, they did not know how to proceed. They did arrange for the Andersons to come over one weekend but it fell through. I do not know if the excuse was real or imagined. They allowed Lindsey to come over but because she was "recovering", her parents insisted that she come home by 8:00 p.m. again.

Our first few nights back in my room we were like strangers trying to get to know each other. Finally, Lindsey told me that her parents were afraid for her because of the hereditary illness she had and since not enough was known about it, they were afraid that excitement, stress, lack of sleep, or anything unusual might trigger it and they would lose their daughter. Lindsey told me she felt hemmed in by a growing wall of fear that she did not know how to counteract. She tried talking to her parents about it but they were afraid to tell her the real reason for fear it would scare her. So everyone in her house knew but her parents did not know that Lindsey knew.

We debated on how to talk to her parents but could not come to any conclusions. Finally, she looked at her watch. It was 7:30 p.m. She came over to the chair next to my wheelchair and said, "I've missed you. I want you to know that I think you were brave in trying to defend me. I don't blame you for what happened, Jimmy."

A great sense of relief washed over me. Lindsey never lied about her feelings. She had learned from her dad not to hide her fear or anger because it only made you worse inside. She saw the look of relief on my face. "Do you blame yourself?"

I nodded. Of course, I blamed myself! I was the person who was supposed to protect her. I had failed. Not only that, but my temper made the situation worse than it should have been.

"Don't change, Jimmy," she pleaded. "I don't want you to change in that you become over-protective of me like my parents have. Please." She looked at me with those brown eyes. I felt better.

"Okay." I promised.

She kissed me.

That was something I had been longing to do. When we finished kissing it was time for her to go home.

I finally remembered what Lindsey wanted to show me that night at the prom. I went to the web site she had mentioned and read about an American doctor who had success reversing spinal cord injuries. Unfortunately, the American Medical Association did not approve of the practice so this doctor had moved his spinal cord clinic to Brazil.

I read seven or eight testimonies of patients who were paraplegics like me and who had recovered full use of their limbs. The process took a number of years but only one surgery. I got the phone number of a couple of patients whose testimonies were on the web site and called them.

"You would be a perfect candidate," one of them told me. "I was injured when I was seventeen and Doctor Lang did the surgery when I was twenty-four. You would have a better chance of recovery than I did!"

All the patients I managed to contact over the next week told me how wonderful the clinic was but most importantly, they told me that it had really worked; they were walking. Some of them with canes, but all of them were out of their wheelchairs!

When I had enough information, I began talking about it with some of my professors at school. Only one had heard about the surgery. The others discounted the testimonies as faith healing mumbo jumbo. The one professor who had heard of it though, encouraged me to look into it. He suggested that I contact the doctor and see if he thought I was a candidate or not.

Lindsey was excited when she learned that I was actually looking into this. I asked her to sit down with me that night while I explained it to my parents and asked for their blessing. She readily agreed and asked her parents for permission to eat supper at my house.

After supper, my mom cleared the table with Lindsey's help and then we sat down and I began to explain what I had learned. My mom and dad were at first skeptical but then began to ask questions. By 8:00 that evening, we had agreed that my dad would contact the doctor for an appointment just to see if I was a candidate for the procedure. My mom was cautiously excited. She did not say so but I could see hope in her eyes for the first time since the accident.

"What if it goes badly?" She wanted to know, "Will things get worse?"

I could not answer that question but I promised it was something we would ask the doctor.

My dad made an appointment with the doctor the next day. He was going to be in Dallas for a short time and agreed to give us two hours and an appointment at his clinic. My mom insisted on going with my dad and me. I tried not to think about it for fear of disappointment.

That night I sat thinking. My life would be so different. My first fifteen years of life I'd pretty much wasted. I was a selfish, boring jock with an attitude. That life ended when the deer ran in front of the car. My new life did not begin until Lindsey poked her head into my bedroom. If I could walk again, what would I do?

A thrill of anticipation raised the hair on my neck. I would definitely get to experience the one pleasure denied to me by the injury! I rolled over to the window. "You'd be a whole man, Jimmy," I whispered to my reflection in the double-thick glass.

I imagined Lindsey's reproach, and it was as palpable as if she had been standing in front of me. I had not thought of anyone but myself when I uttered that sentence. Ashamed,

I rolled away from the window and over to the computer. She needed me to think about her now, not myself!

I typed *Meckler's Disease* into the search engine at my computer. Nothing came up. I switched search engines and tried again. Still nothing. I tried every trick in the book but there were no articles on this rare disease.

"How do doctors know about it?" I asked myself. "How did the doctor at the hospital diagnose the disease if it's so rare?" My room remained silent except for the churning fan on the computer. I wheeled around the room, looking at the full bookshelves. None of the books from my first year of college had anything about the disease. I went back to the computer.

After an hour, I gave up. I had to go to bed.

The next morning, I woke up early with a thought. I'd heard about a search engine called "Dog Pound" that ignored the routine search and went about looking for topics a totally different way. I brought it up and typed in "Meckler."

Two thousand articles and web sites popped up. I looked at the clock. We were leaving soon. I refined the search to Meckler's. The dog symbol on the search engine wagged its tail. A dozen articles showed up. The middle article's blue underlined header declared, "A rare, hereditary disease with no known cure..."

I printed it and got ready for the trip to Dallas.

On the airplane, I read the article. It was an experimental treatment using drugs developed from—and this sent chills up and down my spine—the Cataleya Orchid! The coincidence was mind-boggling. Best of all, the article mentioned by name the doctor who was doing the research. The article mentioned an island in Hawaii I had never heard of. I put the article away.

I wasted no time in writing a letter. I had to address it to Dr. Laird in care of the magazine because the location details were rather nebulous.

As I sat back and considered all of this good news, I had a weird chill. So many things could interfere! First, of course is that the research on the orchid would prove to be worthless. Second, Lindsey's parents would absolutely refuse to have anything to do with an experimental treatment. Third, those idiots at Lindsey's school would cause her more trouble creating the kind of stress that might trigger the disease. Fourth...

I found myself despondent and worried. Lindsey would not approve of my pessimism—that was for sure. Another thought worried me; lately Lindsey had grown withdrawn and quiet. I knew her parents were scared...please don't let it affect Lindsey! I could feel my heart begging for just one miracle that would match the miracle of Lindsey in my life.

Chapter 10

With mom and dad at my side, I flew to Dallas to keep the appointment with Dr. Lang. He did an examination, looked at my charts and X-rays and then sat down with all of us in his plush office. When he finished explaining everything and answering questions, he told us he had an opening in two months time. It was the last opening he had until next April. He agreed to hold the slot open for forty-eight hours.

We went back to the hotel room and talked it over. It would cost $30,000 for the three weeks in Brazil and another $10,000 for the therapy afterwards. Insurance would not cover the cost. He mentioned that in the United States this procedure would cost over $100,000 because insurance would pay the bills and the cost of medical care was three times what it needed to be. In Brazil, we would have the same sterile operating room but drugs, nursing, and hospital costs were so much lower. The drawback, and the reason for the AMA's reluctance, was that only fifty percent of the patients undergoing this surgery had positive outcomes. There was a chance that my recovery would be incomplete. If for some reason, the spinal cord did not regenerate I might end up with intense pain but no positive benefits. Only thirteen percent of his patients had that result and nobody under the age of thirty. In the end, we accepted the offer and the appointment. Dad wrote a check and we made arrangements. With a summer surgery, I would not have to miss any time in school if after surgery things went well.

Lindsey saw us drive in and hurried over to the house. She could barely control her excitement when I reported what the doctor said. "Just think! You could be walking soon! I'm so excited!" She threw her arms around my neck and hugged me.

"It's not that easy," I warned her. "There's a fifty percent chance it won't work at all. And there is a smaller chance that I could get the pain but no benefit."

"That won't happen!" She glared at me. "Stop thinking like that!"

I grinned at her.

Things got worse at the Anderson house. It seemed as though Lindsey's step dad took a greater interest in our relationship and in his stepdaughter. He had never been as interested before and that was fine with Lindsey. He was a kind, patient man who loved her and her mom. Now, Lindsey thought, with her mom pushing the buttons, her step dad was finding things that they had to do as a family. All that meant was Lindsey could not spend as much time with me as we had grown accustomed to. When she did come over, her eyes came alive again while we talked about the treatments, about Meckler's Disease and our future. However, she clouded up again when it was time to go home.

Instead of spending every day and weekends together now, the Andersons had squeezed her time so tightly that she and I barely had two days together and then only until 8:00 p.m.

Just before school ended for the summer, Lindsey lost a chess match to someone that she had beaten every time in the past. She told me she was not as sharp as when we had time to play each other. The chess club members stopped coming to my house because Lindsey asked them to stay away. She wanted uninterrupted time with me since it was so rare anymore.

I decided to talk to the Andersons. My parents encouraged me in that and even arranged an appointment with Lindsey's mom and dad. I plucked up my courage and wheeled over to their house one evening at the appointed time. My heart knocked in my chest because this was a very unusual thing for me. I was used to confronting people when I was angry and I needed that to fuel my words. I could not be angry with the Andersons and so I had very little to go on except conviction.

I knocked on the door and Mr. Anderson opened it. He motioned for me to come in. I wheeled into the house, feeling the tension. Mr. Anderson directed me to the living room and then sat down on the couch next to his wife. She had come from the kitchen and was wiping her hands with a towel as I wheeled into the room. We sat in the living room, Lindsey's mom and step-dad on the couch, Lindsey and I on the other side of the room.

Lindsey sat down next to me, slipped her fingers into mine, and squeezed. I suddenly felt more confident. The conversation was stilted and awkward while we tried to get comfortable. At last, I cleared my throat and began. "I don't know if you remember much about me when you first moved here, but I was a lot different then," I said by way of preamble. "I hated the whole world because I felt that my life had been taken away from me. I didn't care who I hurt because I'd allowed myself to get angry at everything and everyone."

I took a deep breath. Lindsey's fingers felt good, secure, and comfortable in my hand. "I don't know if you remember those days." I looked up. To my surprise, they nodded. They did remember them.

Lindsey's mom said softly, "Lindsey came home from your house crying that first week." Her pain-filled eyes were a shock to me. The memory still hurt Lindsey's mom.

I looked at Lindsey in surprise. I saw the truth in her eyes. Instead of hurt or anger now, I saw love. My heart swelled. Her look told me that she believed in me, trusted me, and knew that my being here tonight would make a difference. I hoped so. It was a lot to live up to.

I looked back at her mom. "Why did you let her come back?"

Mrs. Anderson shrugged, a tiny smile played at the corners of her mouth. "She's quite independent. She grew up differently than most girls. She insisted that you were the one who was hurt, not her. She insisted that she was crying for you, not because you hurt her." I saw the memory of pain in Mrs. Anderson's eyes.

I looked at the soft, delicate, wonderful hand in my hand. "I wouldn't have gone back to school, Mrs. Anderson, if not for Lindsey. I could not believe her courage. For the last five years I've been trying to live in the kind of courage that she demonstrates daily." Tears trickled down my cheeks. It is a terrible thing to find out about the pain you have caused others to endure. I pressed on, "I'm not as good at telling you what I feel as I am at feeling it. I'm sorry. And, I'm so sorry for the pain I caused both of you and Lindsey back then." I dabbed at my face.

Lindsey handed me a Kleenex. I looked up in time to see Mrs. Anderson wipe something from her cheek. "I made a mistake at the Prom. Maybe those boys were not going to hurt her, but I could not take that chance. It was a freak accident that wouldn't have happened if I wasn't in a wheelchair." I spoke bitterly now. "I'm so sorry I couldn't protect her! I would gladly give my life for her, Mr. and Mrs. Anderson. I promise that!"

Mr. Anderson put a hand on his wife's arm. She looked at him. It was his turn to speak. "Linda and I appreciate all that you have been through," he said kindly. "We believe that you have had a very positive impact on Lindsey, uh, after the first year."

He took a deep breath. Now the bad news: I steeled myself and Lindsey's fingers tightened in my hand. "There's no doubt that she has gone beyond the call of duty to help you." I felt suddenly chilled. That did not sound positive. Lindsey felt it too. "We think it is time that she opened up her horizons a bit." His voice became earnest. They had discussed this at some length. This was rehearsed and thoughtful. "Lindsey has been rather sheltered in her relationships. We think that she needs some time away from you so she can get her bearings and get a different perspective."

"Mom, what are you saying?" Lindsey had promised to let me talk but neither one of us expected this. She addressed the question to her mom because she guessed Mr. Anderson had simply been elected spokesman.

Her mother swallowed. She looked at me. "We're not saying that you haven't been a good influence lately, Jimmy. We just think Lindsey needs to have other experiences." She looked at her husband for help. It wasn't going as easily as they had hoped.

He cleared his throat. I could feel Lindsey's hand tightening in the same way that it was kneading my shoulder that night at the prom. I tightened my fingers back trying to warn her to stop and let them finish what they had to say. "All she's known is the distance between our house and your house, Jimmy," he said. "We think that she's been tied down a little..." He looked at me. "Can you understand what we are trying to say?"

I nodded once. I did understand. It made sense that Lindsey had made up her mind before seeing more of the possibilities and opportunities that lay ahead of her.

The girl next to me rewarded me with a frown for capitulating. I could feel through her fingers that she was getting ready for battle. Her heart was pounding in her fingertips, so I knew she was not as calm as she looked. She lowered her gaze for a moment as she tried to form her response.

"When dad died, and we lived alone for two years, I learned a lot about myself," she began.

I settled back in the wheelchair. As tense as the moment was, I knew I was about to learn something about Lindsey and that excited me.

"I was nine when he died. I realized how short life can be." She squeezed my hand. I knew she was thinking of the blood clot too. "My dad loved me, but he was never happy with his life. It was inside him..."

She saw the look on her mother's face and added quickly, "...nothing could make him happy because he wasn't happy down here." She pointed to a spot mid-way on her chest. "I don't want to live for tomorrow—always hoping for something that will make me happy. I am determined to live each day to its fullest, because I might not have another." She wiped a tear from her cheek.

I was awe-struck. Lindsey's approach to life suddenly made sense; her hunger for learning, her happiness, and her desire to include others in that life. All of these things were an outcome of her desire to live each day to the fullest.

"I have been happy, mom. I'm not afraid that I'm missing out on life. I have lots of friends. I'm doing what I love to do. I'm happy." She looked at her mom.

Mrs. Anderson swallowed hard. She drew a breath and looked at her husband. She was wavering in her resolve. I could see it and so could Mr. Anderson. He met her gaze and raised a single eyebrow. Lindsey's mom turned back to her daughter. "I know that seems true now, honey, but you don't know that for sure. You have nothing to compare..." she lost her train of thought as Lindsey reacted.

Lindsey's fingers tensed. I knew I was about to experience something I'd never seen before. She was going to erupt and I could not stop her.

"I haven't been tied down, mom! I've never been as free as I have the last few years." Her mom started to interrupt but Lindsey plunged on, "It's only been recently, since the accident, that I've been tied down!" She broke into tears from the sheer effort of trying to make her mom and step dad understand. "I've been very happy, mom. I love Jimmy! I love living next door to the Turners. But since the prom it seems like I've been trapped and restricted and tied down by some invisible fear." She choked up and could not continue.

"Don't you talk..." Mr. Anderson started to reprimand Lindsey but his wife put a restraining hand on his arm.

"We're trying to do what's best for you! Don't you see that?"

"I can't see anything but your fear," Lindsey replied. She spoke simply, honestly.

The Andersons looked at each other. Finally Mrs. Anderson spoke. "I know this is difficult for you, Lindsey and Jimmy. We want you to break it off; we really do." Her face revealed the inner turmoil she felt.

My heart caved. I did not think it was going to keep beating. Lindsey's hand was so tight in mine that my fingers hurt. She was shaking and sobbing. Her mother looked determined and her step dad was poised to intervene if he had to.

There was nothing more to say. I did not know how to salvage this discussion. It was clear from the start that they were ready for me and had already determined the outcome. Lindsey was sixteen, and she was their daughter.

I started to uncurl my fingers from Lindsey's hand but she refused to let me go. Tears slid down her cheeks as she tried to regain her composure. When she was able, she spoke softly but I heard new strength behind her words.

"Mom, dad, I know you are scared and that's why you decided to try to break Jimmy and me up." She looked at her mom. I glanced over and saw her brows knit in concentration. "I've lived in fear before and so have you. I cannot believe that you have forgotten everything we learned then. I will never forget the things my father taught me. He didn't mean to teach me those things but he drummed them into me from the time I could understand." She took a breath. Her fingers tightened in mine. "I'm going to say something to you that comes from the bottom of my heart. I want you to know that I use it now because I am as scared as I ever was when my father was drunk and mean."

She took another breath. "O'Reilly's rabid rabbits are raging tonight."

Her mom's face showed confusion and then went white. She got off the couch and rushed over to Lindsey. She was crying before she got there. She and Lindsey grabbed and clung to each other as if the world was collapsing around them. Mr. Anderson looked at me dumbfounded.

Mrs. Anderson repeatedly brushed her daughter's hair with her hand. She kissed her fiercely and looked at me.

With tears in her eyes and wet streaks down her face she said, "I'm sorry, Jimmy. I'm so sorry."

Waves of relief threatened to overwhelm me. Mr. Anderson looked like he wanted to get out of the nut house.

It was a long time before Mrs. Anderson went back to the couch and patted her husband's arm. "I'll tell you later," she said. She looked at Lindsey. "Let's get the men something to drink, okay?"

When the women came back from the kitchen with cokes Lindsey looked at me with red-rimmed eyes that had never been so beautiful. Why is it that girls look so much better than boys do when they have been crying? It is probably because we do not have much practice at it.

We sipped our cokes and tried to think of a topic that might be mutually interesting. I did not want to get into an emotional discussion. "Has Lindsey told you about the surgery?" I asked conversationally.

Mrs. Anderson visibly tensed and then forced herself to relax. "Lindsey's told us some things," she said cautiously.

I babbled for a while about the arrangements and the hopes we had for a full recovery based on the testimonies of the people I had talked to. Only after I told her about the chance for me to walk again did I feel like it was disconcerting to her but it did not really register. Lindsey and I talked while they made smiling faces in response.

Lindsey tried to interject a little humor in because she saw the tenseness too. "Don't worry, mom. I'll still be faster than he is."

I laughed.

Finishing the cokes was my clue to leave. The Andersons allowed Lindsey to walk outside with me. She bent down for a goodnight kiss. We talked and held hands for a few minutes. I wheeled home thinking how pretty, smart and caring she was; and how lucky I was.

Later that night, I realized that I had spoken of my hope and future in glowing terms but all they could see was their daughter's disease. That explained their smiling faces without genuine joy. It wasn't because they were upset that I might get better. They were upset that Lindsey might never have the future that she desired—and deserved.

❖❖❖

Lindsey once again had permission to be with me. It was grudging, Lindsey thought, but the restrictions were off. She had fully recovered from her injury. She threw herself into catching up on the work she missed at school. Her junior year was ending and she had a lot of catching up to do.

I loved glancing over at her as she studied. She seemed serene. She loved knowledge. She had just begun talking about going into psychiatry when she graduated high school. I thought she would be the best psychiatrist anyone could have. I could not help but admire her with every breath I took.

❖❖❖

Just before I left for Brazil Lindsey came over. I could see her eyes were red from crying. My heart lurched inside me. I did not need bad news before I made this trip. It was possible that something had flared up because of injury to her spleen or there was some news about Meckler's disease that was terrible. I steeled myself for the worst. I was frightened enough. I found myself fearing she had lost her optimism.

"Sorry," she said when she saw me looking at her eyes. "I'm happy, that's all. I'm not worried." But she broke down and leaked fresh tears. We were alone so I pulled her onto my lap and rested my chin on her shoulder while she regained her composure. Her hair was in ponytails, one on each side.

"You are a little worried, though, aren't you?" I asked when she stopped crying.

She denied it by shaking her head. Her ponytails slapped me on both sides of my face. I reached up and turned her face toward mine.

Her kisses were soft and sweet. Neither one of us had ever kissed anyone else. I could not conceive of kissing another girl—except my mom and that was different! Lindsey's kisses were special, mood altering kisses. I could not stay upset or hurt or angry when she kissed me because she knew exactly how long to kiss depending on where I hurt or how happy we were. I cannot explain it. Moreover, when it was over, it was not over. Her kisses lingered long past the time she went home. I could feel her breath on my cheek, her lips against mine and sometimes I went to sleep tasting those kisses. This kiss was sweeter, tenderer, more filled with love than any other kiss I had ever experienced. Her kisses came straight from her heart to my lips and shot electricity through my body—the parts I could feel. Think of how intense kisses are when you can feel them in your feet! I could not, so the kisses that should have gone to my feet piled up in my stomach and chest and lungs and fingertips! Oh how I loved kissing her!

When she pulled away, she got up and sat down across from me. She looked into my eyes. "I believe in this," she said. "I believe with all my heart that it is going to work for you. Last night I laid awake thinking how wonderful it is

going to be to stand with you and hold you in my arms..."
her face contorted but she managed to quell the tears. "But
it doesn't matter to me Jimmy! It doesn't matter. Standing,
lying, running, walking...it is all the same. I'm content just
being with you."

We held each other for a long time.

It was hot in Tennessee the afternoon we left on
Continental Airlines from the Nashville airport. I dreaded
the long hours and the inconvenience. We changed planes
in Miami at 5:12 p.m. After a three-hour layover that seemed
endlessly long, we lifted off and crossed the South Atlantic
Ocean. The trip was night travel and we tried to sleep. My
mom and dad sat next to me and did what they could to
make the flight more comfortable. A flight attendant took
an interest in us and brought us everything we needed. It
helped.

We landed at 5:00 a.m. in the morning just as the sky
was getting light without a visible sun in it. It was going to
be a scorcher in Sao Paulo so we were grateful to get to our
hotel with minimal delay. A forty-five-minute taxicab ride
to the center of the city, which had sprung to life, brought us
to the *Tryp Campinas* hotel. I could not wait to tell Lindsey
about it. The lobby was magnificent. The floor was marble
and all desks, counters, and walls were made of the same
type and grade of marble. A huge white marble staircase
rose from the center of the lobby to a balcony above where
alcoves for private meetings gave people a view of the lobby
below and a view of the awakening city outside. Our room
had two king-size beds and was equipped with handicapped
facilities better and more modern than any I had seen in
the States. I was only going to be in the room for a day to
rest up before transferring to the clinic a block away. I was
too excited to rest much so I wandered around looking at

the sights. People were friendly and seemed more at ease with handicapped people. By noon, I was exhausted and ready for sleep.

The clinic was in a modern high-rise medical center with state of the art equipment and facilities. I was expecting a third-world style medical center with dirt floors and antique equipment and was relieved the moment I saw the place. My mom and dad were relieved too, so I know they secretly had harbored the same fears. Dr. Lang introduced us to the staff, Maria and Ling would be my nurses. We toured the operating room that was stainless steel and as modern as any I had seen. With the surgery scheduled for the next morning at 9:00 a.m., Maria and Ling took me to my hospital room.

The room was set up the way you would want your bedroom to be set up if you were handicapped. Everything was accessible and easy to use. Even the bed could be raised and lowered electrically to suit the height of the patient. It was a lot more comfortable than my room at home and I was very comfortable in my room!

Alone in my hospital room to wait for morning, I decided to write down my love for Lindsey just in case. I grabbed a pad of paper and a pen from the table and tried to think how to begin. I wasted an hour and six or seven sheets of paper before I finally found myself on the right track.

> *Lindsey*
> *I'm not sure I can tell you what I feel. My language ability seems inadequate when it comes to writing these kinds of letters: letters that are necessary because we are physically apart. One thing you never knew, and I want you to know now, is what you did to me about four years ago.*

Remember the time you came back from vacation and didn't even go into your house? You came right over so you could tell me about your vacation. You ran across the yard just to see me. We'd known each other for one year and I had grown to like you. I'm a little embarrassed to admit this, so bear with me. Don't show this to anyone! Anyway, I guess I'm really feeling like I need to remember everything about you right now. I'm hungry because I can't eat anything before surgery and I'm lonely because this place is shutting down for the night...okay, but please! You came running across the yard and I felt a thrill go through me. It was totally unexpected that you would be so anxious to see me. I listened to every sound in the house to see if I could tell that you were anxious to see me or just trying to get out of unloading the car (ha). The front door opened, my mom gave you a hug and you flew up the steps. I heard every footstep and you were hurrying. Oh, Lindsey! I felt so good. I think you remember me teasing you about your Bawstahn accent...but what really happened was I noticed for the first time that you were growing up. Your chest gave you away. And, when you left to go back and help unload, you brushed my cheek with a kiss. How come I can still see you and feel the feather-light touch of that kiss here in Sao Paulo?

One thing I know for sure is that you love me. I can tell by the way you want to sit near me in the car. I feel complete when you put your head on my shoulder and your long, brown hair that smells so good, falls onto my chest. I'm in the hospital here in Brazil, over a thousand miles from you and I can smell your hair. Isn't that silly? Truthfully, I'm scared—until I remember the way you looked at me with such transparent belief that this was the right thing for me...for us...no, that's not true. Lindsey, I'm

here because I want to be whole when I marry you, if
you will have me, no matter how long it takes or how
many obstacles appear in our way.
I don't want to lose any more time. One of these days,
if this surgery works, I'm going to stand up and let you
put your arms around me while I put mine around
you. It's probably nothing to someone who hasn't lived
in a wheelchair as long as I have. Right now it seems
like that would be the greatest gift I could receive.
I love you, Lindsey.

I folded the letter and sealed it into an envelope. I
scribbled Lindsey's name on it and put it on the table. Then
it was morning. My mom and dad came early and we talked
about nothing and everything. It was the kind of talk you
do when you are nervous but don't want to talk about being
nervous. They told me about the weather, about talking to
my nurses—who I had not seen since they tucked me into
bed. They told me about breakfast and then about supper
the previous night. It made my stomach growl.

Maria and Ling came in. They put an IV in after
scrubbing the back of my hand raw with an alcohol pad!
The doctor came in as they were gowning me and he talked
to us while Maria painted my back with purple liquid. Dr.
Lang said we were ready to go and that he would report to
my parents when I was in recovery.

They shifted me to another bed and rolled me onto
my stomach. The last thing I noticed was Maria sticking
a syringe into the IV line. I woke up twelve hours later.
The first faces I saw were Maria and Ling and then I saw
my mom, dad, and what seemed like minutes later, Dr.
Lang. I could make out that he was talking but could not
hear or understand his words. I thought he was talking in
Spanish or Portuguese. My parents told me later that he

was describing the surgery and explaining to them how well it had gone.

I had to stay in bed at the hospital for the next two and a half weeks. I got to know Maria and Ling. They were conscientious and attentive. Ling was from China and Maria was from Mexico. Ling spoke Portuguese with such a funny accent that Maria sometimes told her to speak in English so she could understand her. I felt no pain from the surgery. They took a donor graft from my leg and the doctor told me I would have a battle scar. I would have a scar on my back too, but I already had one from the accident. Maria and Ling exercised my legs three and four times a day after the surgery. They made me do pull ups to keep my strength up and chided me when I did not eat as much as I should.

Lindsey's parents took vacation, back to the Boston area, and Lindsey went with them while I was in Brazil. She wrote to me every day. I got her letters and cards in bunches because of the mail system. It did not matter. I was happy to get them.

I wrote back and Maria mailed my postcards and letters for me the first week. When I did not know if Lindsey would get them because she was on vacation, I kept them. I sealed each one separately and asked my mom put them in my suitcase.

At last, the time came to return to the states. The flight home was exhausting. Lindsey was waiting when the ambulance my dad hired to bring me from the airport drove into our driveway. She waited with my parents while the attendants put me into bed. When all that was over, she kissed me and hugged me. Her hair tickled my face and it was the best feeling in the world. Before she left, I gave her the letter I had written and told her to read it at home.

I forgot about the dozen other letters I had written and did not remember them until after she left.

I gathered that she liked my letter from the look in her eyes when she came back the next day after reading it.

"I almost ran over here last night after I read this letter!" She bent down and brushed my cheek with her lips. "Is that the kind of kiss you remember?"

I nodded.

"We've kissed a few times since that one," she said.

"I know, but that one meant so much...I didn't really explain it very well in the letter. People kiss for many reasons. You didn't have to kiss me at all. None of the reasons I could think of were good enough to explain that kiss except that you liked me a lot. I didn't like myself! You liked me more than I liked myself!" I was babbling.

Lindsey's eyes were bright. She leaned down and kissed me on the lips.

Over the next few days, Lindsey helped my mom by exercising my legs as the doctor prescribed. Those were some great times together.

Every day during my mandatory convalescent time, Lindsey came over and read, played chess and spent hours talking to me. Since it was summer and I was pinned down, so to speak, she had me all to herself. I was happy when it was over and I could get back into the wheelchair. At least life would get back to normal for a while. I was ready!

Things were tenser with her parents than I would have expected. I thought they would be happy for me and encourage me but they were mute on the subject of my surgery. They came over a few times to play games and things seemed to be relaxed a little more each time. I knew they wished me well; it just would have been nice to hear it from them.

Lindsey grew at least another inch. It was hard to judge when you are stuck at four feet. It did seem like she had to bend further to kiss me and that caused another revelation. She had grown up in more than height!

Without any feeling below the waist, my relationship with Lindsey was...different. I appreciated her growing beauty with my eyes and my heart. Before my accident, I was a normal fifteen-year-old and the way I viewed girls was from the waist up. (Not their waist—mine) After the accident, one of the guys who used to be my friend smuggled a Playboy into my room. He thought it would be funny, I guess or maybe he just did not think. I was so depressed about the accident and my lot in life that I threw the magazine away after glancing at the pictures. I could not tell if they excited me or not. That one incident probably caused my former jock friends and me to part ways. They came back to tease me and talk dirty and I kicked them out.

That is why I was mad at the world. I had no interest in girls. That is why it was so remarkable that Lindsey made it past my defenses. Perhaps because she was just eleven, going on twelve at the time I did not see her as a threat—a reminder of my incapacity. She was like an annoying sister that you loved to hate. A pest that turned out to have more brains than any two kids I ever met in my life! Moreover, when I met her, I was four feet tall. She was taller than I was.

When I made it back into my wheelchair, she bent down to kiss me the first time, the neck of her shirt hung down, and I got a glimpse of...well, I would describe it but it is private. Suffice it to say she was not wearing a bra. Anyway, it astounded me and I almost could not close my lips to kiss her!

She noticed too. She apologized and then kissed me again—only this time she held her hand against the top of her shirt to keep it from acting like a peep show. I had a touch more passion in my kiss than I could ever remember. When she sat down across from me, my eyes kept straying to her tee shirt. When she went home that night, I could not get that picture out of my mind. I finally decided my life was quite full and wonderful because I could admire her physical beauty as well as the inner beauty that I had come to respect and love since we met. Still, I could not help but think that maybe, if the miracle happened, I would...I put it out of my mind and went to sleep.

The next day she wore a bra and apologized for the mistake. "I take you for granted," she said holding my hand. "I forget about stuff like that," she said awkwardly.

"Look," I said, "It's just that I was startled. I've been taking you for granted too. I've been admiring your mind and your spirit for four years and I forgot that you were growing more beautiful in other ways too."

She smiled so sweetly that it made the back of my throat hurt. It made me realize in that moment she was a woman and had been waiting for me to tell her that I found her to be beautiful, not just brainy. I kicked myself for being a dumb klutz. It seems like I become aware of things suddenly only to realize they have been there all along. Her expression of delight warmed my heart. Then she spoke the most beautiful words a woman can give a man, "I love you, Jimmy Turner!" Our kiss lasted a long time.

There is nothing like physical therapy. I had three sessions a week starting August first, only a couple of days after I got back into my wheelchair. Doctor Lang did not want to waste any time. After thirty minutes the first time out I was completely spent. The braces that now stabilized me instead of a titanium rod in my back were a lot less comfortable if my skin was any judge. Here's a hint: use *Udder Cream* for the sores. I got into bed at night—and had to lie on a very hard mattress to keep my spine straight when I took the braces off. Anyway, hot packs, cold packs, ultrasound, and one or more types of electrical stimulation followed the hard work in therapy sessions.

I felt none of the physical therapy in my legs, even though that was where the therapist was concentrating, but I did feel it in my chest, lungs, and heart. I did not mind the swimming pool sessions but the parallel bars and attempting to walk was murder on my shoulders.

August was hot but with our birthdays coming up, I wanted to do something special for Lindsey. Because of what the therapy consisted of, I suddenly had an idea and my therapist, thankfully, went along with it. I asked Lindsey to go with me to the next therapy session, which happened to fall on her birthday. I told her we would do something after therapy but I really wanted her to come. She agreed and rode with me to the University. I kept looking at her and finally she gave me that quizzical look that I did not need translated into words.

"Do you know how tall I am?" I asked.

She looked at me. It was rare to catch her off guard. I could see her trying to estimate, then the light of humor came into her eyes, and she said, "About four feet, one inch."

"Funny," I said.

She loosened her seat belt and slid over on the seat next to me. She fastened the center belt and kissed my cheek. "You're the right size for me, Jimmy." She snuggled against me.

We talked about my research, and I could see that the
discussion invigorated her. She really wanted to know about
Meckler's Disease. "I haven't found any more research on
it since that weird thing about the flower," I told her.

"And he hasn't written back to you?"

"Not a word."

"What about Chuck's brother, Steve, the doctor?"

"Oh shoot! I need to call him."

"Do you think he knows anything?"

"I'm not sure, really. I'm hoping he can help guide me
in this research. Plus, I have to have a mentor next year.
I figure that if Chuck's brother wouldn't mind, he could
mentor me too."

"That's a great idea." Lindsey's brown hair was done
up in a bun. I had never seen it like that except on formal
occasions. I much preferred it hanging loose because it was
so pretty.

I took my hand off the controls and put my arm around
her shoulders. She snuggled against me. The long, straight
highway did not require two hands on the wheel. I loved the
way she felt against me. I guess what I loved the most was
how she seemed to love me so fiercely. She never missed a
chance to be with me. She challenged me because she was a
thinker who did not accept anything at face value. She saw
through my moods and left me alone when that was the
wiser course of action. And she was beautiful.

We rode in silence for so long that I thought she might
be sleeping. I could not wait for the day when I would wake
up in my bed and she would be smiling at me. Or maybe she
would be asleep and I would thrill as she opened her eyes
and then smiled when she saw me. Instead of the triangle
above my bed, I wanted Lindsey's face to be the first thing
I saw in the morning!

The physical therapy section was by itself—away from the hustle and bustle of normal campus life. That helped with the parking problem. Even though I had the handicapped-parking pass, it was just pleasant to be away from student drivers trying to get a place at the last minute. A wheelchair rider is not very easy to see when you are a half-asleep teenager with a souped-up car rushing to catch a parking spot.

Lindsey followed me in. The receptionist smiled at me and pushed the buzzer to let me into the therapy rooms. I punched the blue button and the doors swung open. I wheeled down the hallway. Matt, my trainer, was waiting. He shook hands with Lindsey and gave me a look that made me want to punch him and happy that he was so envious at the same time.

"I'm going to get Jimmy ready." He handed her a tape measure. "Hold on to this." He saw the question in her eyes. "Jimmy's request," he grinned at her.

Matt positioned me in the harness and then helped me stand between the parallel bars. I gripped them and progressively "walked" up the incline until my feet were flat and my legs were straight. Then Matt adjusted the harness that stabilized me and called Lindsey to come over.

Lindsey had been watching my progress with a great deal of interest. She got up quickly and came to stand beside me. She handed the tape measure to Matt. He took it and then asked her to come around the parallel bars. He guided her to the other end. At once, she understood what he wanted and stepped up between the bars and came to stand in front of me. When she stopped in front of me, we were standing face-to-face for the first time. The top of her head came to my chin. It thrilled me when she looked *up* to see my face. "So how do I look," I asked quietly.

"Tall," she replied. The smile on her face matched mine.

Matt muttered, "Happy birthday!" Then he turned and nearly ran out of the room.

I grinned at Lindsey. I was supporting my weight with my arms but I felt comfortable. I'd held myself in this position for fifteen minutes during therapy sessions while I dragged my legs "walking."

"Happy Birthday, Lindsey," I said softly. Then I leaned forward to kiss her on the lips. Lindsey unhesitatingly raised her lips to mine. When the kiss was over, she started to cry tears of joy. I felt a surge of hope go through me. She hugged me and cried all the more because it was the first time she was able to put her arms all the way around me and lay her head on my chest. It was awesome!

Matt gave us five minutes together. I found myself wishing I could put my arms around her in the same way she was holding me. But since it was the first time she had seen me "standing" and the first time I'd been able to lean down and kiss her instead of her leaning down to kiss me, I was happy. I could smell her hair and the scent of the soap she had used that morning and feel the wetness on my chest from her cheeks.

When my therapist walked back into the room, he handed Lindsey the tape measure. She measured me. "Six feet, one inch," she announced, letting the tape scroll back into the container.

Matt helped me get into the chair then and for most of the therapy session, Lindsey watched from the bench. When Matt put the electric stimulation pads on my legs Lindsey came over and held my hand. She pretended that she was getting the buzzing sensation and we laughed together. She sat on the floor near my bench and kissed me on the nose. "This was nice," she said softly.

I murmured something sappy. She kissed my nose again, got up, and went back to the bench because Matt was coming over to take the instruments of torture off me. When she was out of earshot Matt whispered, "Man, you are one lucky dude!" He meant it too. "How old is she?"

"If I told you that, you might have to kick her out of the therapy room," I said. I gave him a look.

"Ah, man," he said, "Don't tell me you're robbing the cradle. She's older than she looks, right?"

"Yeah," I said. "She *sure* is."

Chapter 11

Back in the university, I worked hard on my studies but I spent every spare moment researching what I came to call Lindsey's Silent Disease. Except for that one ray of hope and the coincidence of the orchid, I found nothing more in the medical journals, internet sites or volumes of text that filled the dusty library shelves. I wrote two more letters to the researcher who had written the article about the Cataleya Orchid, but the semester wore on without a response.

I searched the internet and our library's card catalogue for everything I could find about the Cataleya Orchid. There was nothing linking it to medical research.

Chuck Singleton popped into my mind and I called him. "Chuck, remember after the prom when you told me your brother was an intern at a hospital?"

"Sure, he's a resident now." Chuck was a senior like Lindsey. "He's at Tennessee Medical the teaching hospital."

"Do you think he'd mind if I called him?"

"Hey, go ahead. I'm supposed to call him tonight anyway. I'll give him your number and tell him you want to talk about...?"

"It's about Meckler's Disease."

"Oh, right. Sounds like a terrible chess move like Castling Disease or Rookism."

When I did not laugh he snorted. "Same old Jimmy; okay, okay, I'll tell him."

"Thanks, Chuck. And thanks for showing up in the hallway when you did that night. I don't know what would have happened if you hadn't."

"No problem. Hey, stay in touch."

That night Steve Singleton called me and introduced himself as Chuck's older brother. "Hey, Jimmy. Thanks for what you've done for my brother."

"That's mutual, Dr. Singleton. He actually saved Lindsey's life, did he tell you?"

"He mentioned something about the prom." There was a long pause.

I decided to fill the gap. "Uh, the reason I wanted to talk to you, is one to ask if you would consider mentoring me at Tennessee University and two, to see if you had ever heard of Meckler's Disease."

"When Chuck told me what you wanted I did a little research. There is a mention of that disease in the Physicians' Desk Reference but very little is known about it. Why are you interested in such a rare disease?"

I told him about Lindsey and her father. There was a long silence. Then he said, "Yeah, I'd like to do both, Jimmy."

"Both?"

"Mentor you and try to figure out what's going on with this disease."

That was quick! "Thanks, Doctor!"

"Hey, Jimmy," he said.

"Yes, sir?"

"My name is Steve."

"Yes, sir...Steve."

"When can we get together?"

"Well, I don't need a mentor until next semester really..."

"You want to waste time that's up to you. Now when can we get together?"

"I've got classes on Monday, Wednesday and Thursday from nine 'till three in the afternoon. After that and on Tuesdays and Fridays, I'm home."

"Is Lindsey available?"

"Do you need to do an exam?" I did not think that would be good with her parents not in the loop.

"No...not now anyway," he said. "It may come to that, but right now I just want to talk about her dad and get a little history if I can."

"Sure! We're together most every night. I'll tell her and see what she says."

"How old is Lindsey?"

"She's seventeen." I could hear the intake of breath at the other end of the line.

"Oh..." there was a thoughtful pause. "...what about her parents; are they together on this or in denial?"

"I'm not sure. They won't talk about it with Lindsey. They think she doesn't know about the disease. I guess they don't want to scare her. I would hate to be the one they thought told her! I'm just out of the dog house from what happened at the prom."

"Look, Jimmy," Steve said kindly, "It's going to be almost impossible to do anything with Lindsey. If we do this, it will have to be with her parent's permission. Can you get their permission?"

"Probably not right now," I answered honestly. I only knew this in my gut, not for sure. But my gut was telling me that they wouldn't want their daughter to be subjected to any probing, testing, and so on in some wild hope dreamed up by the crippled boy next door with a savior complex.

Plus, they weren't ready to tell her about the disease so there was little chance of them giving permission.

Steve was quiet for a while. "Right; well, we don't need her actively involved. I do need to ask her some questions about her dad. Do you think you can arrange that? The sooner the better, if that's alright."

"I know I can arrange that." I felt like a conspirator all of a sudden. I also felt like I was going behind the Anderson's backs. That was not something I really wanted to do. But I did want to do everything to help Lindsey even if they were determined to protect and shelter her from the truth. As long as she was with me, I was moving ahead. We had very different views on Lindsey's ability to handle truth—even when it caused stress.

"Okay, then maybe the best thing to do is to meet at your house, informally, just to talk. Like I said, I'm going to be nearby tomorrow night so if we can do it then, that's the best thing."

When I hung up, I felt that things might be moving forward at last. I could not wait to tell Lindsey!

She was cautiously excited. "Do you think he can help us?"

"I don't know," I admitted. "I've got to believe that all of this crazy coincidence is really Someone looking down on us and giving us a shove."

She looked at me. One of the things we had not discussed, and probably should have, was what we believed about Providence, God, and Fate...what we believed about religion. I did not want to begin that discussion now. It was just that, I really believed it was not an accident that I picked the very orchid that someone claimed was a remedy for Meckler's Disease! Up until now, I hadn't thought much about religion. I thought about the orchid and the incident that turned out okay but alerted Lindsey to her disease... well, it was all too much coincidence to be lightly passed by.

The next night we were together in my room. I was watching out the window for Steve's car. Lindsey was pacing nervously around the room.

"Hey," I said softly, "Stop! You're going to have a nervous breakdown."

"I know." She sat down on my bed. "Just think, Jimmy! If you and Steve figure out a cure for this..." She stopped. "It's just a stupid dream. It won't happen in my lifetime!"

"Wait, whoa!" I said. "It's not like you to give up before you start. What's the matter?"

"I just don't want to get my hopes up, Jimmy. I feel bad about recommending the surgery to you. Your mom is walking around on cloud nine, and every time she sees me, she hugs me! What if it doesn't come true? What if you're part of the thirteen percent?"

"She wouldn't blame you," I said.

"I would! Oh, I don't know, Jimmy! Sometimes I just feel like one of us..." she stopped, her face turned a shade whiter.

"We're going to make it...together!" I declared firmly.

"I know we are, Jimmy. It just seems so overwhelming sometimes."

I rolled my wheelchair over to where she was sitting on the edge of my bed. I took her face in my hands and looked into her troubled, beautiful eyes. "I'm the luckiest man alive. You found me five years ago, right here in this room, willing to die. Now I want to live. I'm in love with you—the girl who refused to be run off by anger and fear. I'm hopelessly hooked." I shrugged my shoulders, "There is no cure for this Lindsey Love Disease."

She grinned at me and kissed me. Hope slipped into her face again.

"Aren't you the girl that told me to stop talking like that not too long ago?" I teased.

She nodded sheepishly. "Sorry. It won't happen again." She made a zipper motion with her finger and threw the imaginary key away.

I suddenly remembered the letters I'd written while she was on vacation. I wheeled to my desk and pulled the stack from the drawer. I put them on my lap and brought them to her. Her eyes looked at me in wonder. "I forgot to give these to you," I said. "I couldn't mail them so I decided to wait and give them to you when I got here."

"What are they?"

"Letters I wrote to you while I was in Brazil. Every card you wrote me meant you were thinking about me. Do you know how awesome it was to get a letter from you every day?" I let that sink in. "Well, I wanted you to know that I thought about you every day too."

"Oh, Jimmy," she said as she took the letters. "How do you always manage to do one more unexpected, wonderful thing?" She rifled through them in amazement. "I love you!"

I realized again that I was safe with Lindsey. I could open my heart and lay it in her lap and she would hold it tenderly. I could be awkward and try to show her how much I loved her and she would appreciate it as if I had done it perfectly. I grinned and felt good.

Her face was wet. We did not exactly prepare for company very well. These moments just seemed to pop up at the strangest times and we both took advantage of them—but it probably made everyone else think we were sappier than a couple of humming birds or wooly-headed woodpeckers. I was getting used to tears of happiness. I tried to remember if she ever cried because she was sad.

Then I did remember and it hurt. I had been mean to her when we first met and she leaked tears but bravely wiped them away at age eleven. *Bravely wiped them away*, that phrase described Lindsey through and through. I hurt her in the hospital and she'd cried then.

I did not care if Steve was coming to meet us for the first time. I pulled her face into my chest. After a moment, she lifted her head and kissed me wetly.

"Jimmy," she said. "If you won't die on me, I won't die on you; promise?"

I did not know where that came from and it made me catch my breath. I wanted to ask but I heard a car turn into the driveway below. Steve had arrived.

"I promise, Lindsey." I assumed that she was talking blood clots and Meckler's Disease. Well if promises were all it took, I was more than happy to make the promise.

My mom guided Steve up the steps. Steve had introduced himself as Chuck Singleton's brother. My mom knew Chuck, of course. I could see she was curious about Steve and the purpose of his visit so I asked her to stay. She very quickly sat by Lindsey on the bed. She hugged Lindsey as she looked at Steve and then at me with interest.

I introduced Lindsey to Steve and they shook hands. I wanted to close the blinds in my window because I felt like we were conspiring behind the Anderson's backs. That would not do, though, because I always left them open when Lindsey and I were together in my room. I had told my mom about Meckler's Disease and told her about Steve mentoring me but I hadn't exactly said anything about Steve's help with my research and how Lindsey was involved.

"Oh," Steve said reaching into his jacket pocket and pulling out a folded piece of paper. "I copied this from the PDR..." He saw my mom's quizzical look and amended, "Physicians' Desk Reference." He unfolded the page and read from it.

> *"A rare blood disorder that lies dormant for years. It remains dormant most of a person's life. The trigger is unknown. When activated, the Disease produces a fatal toxin. The onset of the Disease causes severe headaches, cramps, nausea and euphoria. The euphoria is a side effect of lack of oxygen to the brain. Symptoms last from twelve to seventy-two hours before death. There is no known cure. The Disease is named after the first known victim, Herbert Meckler who was diagnosed in 1959 post mortem."*

Steve folded the paper and put it back into his pocket but I reached out my hand and he gave it to me. He looked at the three of us and then turned his attention to Lindsey.

"Jimmy told me a little bit about you," He said. "I'd like to know more. We are dealing with a rare disease here, at least, as far as we know because rare diseases tend to be misdiagnosed until they become better known. "I want to know about your dad, Lindsey."

Lindsey hesitated and looked at me. I gave her an encouraging nod. Her face still had evidence that she had recently been crying but neither Steve nor my mother said anything about it. I understood, though, the reason for my mother hugging her. "I was thinking about my dad the other day, trying to figure out what you might need to know. I just couldn't think of anything." She folded her hands in her lap.

"Just tell me what you know, even if it seems like it's not very much." Steve was one of those doctors that had a good bedside manner. He had the round, wire rimmed glasses and looked like a scholar. He had black hair that flopped to one side more than the other giving him a lopsided look. All in all, the effect was rather nerdy—like and older version of Chuck. But if he was like Chuck, he was a fast learner and very smart.

Lindsey peered into the past. "My dad was tall and thin. I once heard him complain about only being six feet tall so I guess that's how tall he was. He went partially bald by the time I was eight. He had stinky feet." She grinned at that. Steve encouraged her with a nod. "He worked hard." She shrugged. It was such a long time ago and she was so young.

Steve asked her more questions and she was surprised that she knew the answers. Then he asked about her dad's dad. "Did you know your grandpa very well?"

She shook her head. "He died before I was born."

"How old was he?"

Lindsey tried to remember. "It seems like he was young because my dad said something about the funeral. He said 'He was a mean...' she blushed as she quoted her dad, '... son of a bitch but way too young to die. I hope I don't get whatever bit him.'" Lindsey looked up. "I always thought a rattlesnake bit him or when I got older I thought he was referring to the fact that he inherited his anger."

We all nodded. It was logical.

"Do you have any allergies?" Steve asked. He was taking notes on a little pad he pulled out of his pocket.

"I'm allergic to strawberries," Lindsey said.

That was news to me. I made a fervent wish: please let me have a lifetime to get to know all about her!

"What about shellfish?"

Lindsey looked at him. "Is that important because of Meckler's disease?"

Steve shook his head. "I'm just trying to assemble the pieces. I don't know if any of them belong to this puzzle but you have to learn as much as you can if you're going to have even half a chance. Something like this..." He shrugged, "who knows what is important or not?"

Lindsey considered. "I don't know if I am or not. I don't think I've ever eaten shellfish. My mom never cooks fish. That's strange." She grinned at Steve and me. "And we're from Boston!" She shook her head at the irony of it.

"Do you have any allergies to drugs or medicines, that sort of thing?"

She shook her head.

"And your dad...did he have any allergies?"

"I know both of us hated strawberries because we broke out in hives. But I don't know about anything else."

I'd been hoping that Lindsey would stumble across something during the conversation that would make Steve's ears tingle but I began to realize that we'd better be in this thing for the long haul. I wondered how long it took Alexander Fleming to discover penicillin. Then I wondered if it was as urgent for him as finding this cure for Meckler's Disease was for me! Maybe urgency was the key. If so, then I had a head start.

After Steve left, we went down to the kitchen and mom fed us a snack.

"I like him," Lindsey said. "He has a lot of energy."

I liked him too.

⊹⊱⊰⊹

I was not supposed to feel anything for another couple of months yet. I woke up in the middle of the night in January and it felt like a row of ants was crawling up my butt. I used the intercom to call my mom and dad and they rushed up the stairs to my room.

We had to wait until a decent hour to call Dr. Lang who was supposed to be in the Dallas clinic.

"That's exciting!" He said when he heard. He asked a dozen questions and then told me that I was probably healing faster than expected. I hung up the phone and relayed the good news to my parents.

"So when can you walk?" My mom asked.

I laughed. "Maybe tomorrow," I teased her.

"Really?" Then she blushed. "Jimmy! Why would you tease me about something like this?" She looked at my dad who only grinned at her.

"If my spinal cord is starting to grow back together, maybe in another year or two, I should be able to stand up is what he said," I told them.

The tingling in my butt never quit after that. It began to increase until it literally felt like someone was holding an electrode to my skin.

Lindsey came over that afternoon at her usual time. After we talked for a while and my mom left the room, she sat sideways on my lap and put her arms around my neck. "So what's happening?" She asked. "Is there any more information from Steve or Dr. Lang?"

"Not from Steve," I said. "He's doing a ton of research though, and he's given me a list of topics I have to research." I pointed to the desk. A stack of printouts already littered the top of it.

"So?" She asked, curious to know if any of the research had paid off.

"Nothing yet," I admitted. "But there is something that's different."

She twisted around and looked at me. Her eyes positively glowed with interest. Her Boston accent had returned but I did not want to waste any more time so I told her straight up. "My butt started tingling last night."

Lindsey's mouth flew open. She got off my lap and embraced me laughing and crying and trying to dance while she was bending over holding me. At last, she pulled back and looked at me with tear-glistened eyes. "Oh, my gosh!" she exclaimed happily. "It's working!" She paced around the room looking at me and pacing. "Oh man! I'm so happy!"

I nodded.

"I had a dream, Jimmy," she said suddenly. She sat down at the card table and looked at me and then away. "I dreamed you were walking!" She sat down suddenly. "I dreamed it!" She was practically hugging herself, unable to sit still. "I dreamed you rescued me."

I waited.

"It was two nights ago," she said softly. "I dreamed that I fell down the side of a hill showing off or something. You were in the wheelchair and we were out for one of our strolls. The day was really beautiful." She paused in her narrative. "You looked panicky when I fell down and you rolled to the edge but the only way I was going to live was if you got out of your wheelchair. I was going to give up." Her voice filled with awe as she continued. "So you did. You got up. I watched from down below, hanging onto a tiny bush, over the steepest cliff I'd ever seen, as you grimaced and then took a step and another. You got a rope from somewhere close by, tossed it to me and I grabbed it. I had to let go of the bush and that seemed important to me in the dream. But when I did, you pulled me right up."

Tears were streaming down her face. I wanted to get up right then and walk to her. I believed her dream. I was going to walk someday. I thought the part about rescuing her was her hoping for a cure. Maybe, just maybe, Steve and I could stimulate enough interest in Meckler's Disease over the next few years to do just that.

The joy of what was happening in my body mitigated the more painful part of the regeneration. The only time I did not feel the bugs crawling around my butt after that was when I slept.

In August, Dr. Lang agreed to see me. He was coming through Tennessee anyway so he wondered if it would be okay to examine me at Doctor Singleton's office. When Dr. Lang arrived, I introduced the two of them and later they talked about how Steve could help me as my spinal cord and nerves regenerated. Dr. Lang was extremely pleased with my progress. "It's so fast, Jimmy," he said. "I've never seen it move this fast." He scooted back from the table. "It's just been one year," he said. A nurse came in to help me back into my wheelchair. "I can give you something for the crawly sensation," he offered.

I refused. "No thanks. I'm studying and don't want my head cloudy, Doctor Lang."

"Well, congratulations, then."

I asked if he had heard of Meckler's Disease. He gave it a moment's thought and then shook his head. "I don't think so."

I explained about it and he listened. "I come across a lot of weird things in South America," he said. "I'll keep my ears and eyes open. But I wouldn't expect too much."

I began meeting regularly with Steve as my mentor. His task was to introduce me to the world of medicine on a practical level—the patient level. I got to sit in—literally—on patient consults if they gave permission and exams when those were routine. It gave me a real sense of practical medicine.

"Most of the time," Steve said after a day of exams, "the patient's body will heal itself. Antibiotics simply help speed the process up or help the body get its immune system back in shape. The trick is in knowing when the body needs help and what kind of help it needs."

"This Meckler's Disease," I said. "It's hereditary. How can you fight something that's in the genes?"

He shook his head. "You have to understand the human gene." He sat back in the chair and reached into his memory. "Do you know how a virus works? Take the HIV virus for example. It has a couple of proteins. The first protein allows the virus cell to enter the human cell. That's a big step. The next part of the virus, the second protein attacks and takes over the human cell. It sets up its own shop, sort of, like a crab takes up residence in a new shell. The problem with that is...human cells reproduce. Viruses like HIV—called retroviruses—actually create a new gene within the host cell. When the host splits, the new gene splits right along with it and the virus spreads. It doesn't just attack human cells and destroy them; it gets inside and makes copies of itself until it takes over the body—like HIV." He looked at me.

"So to fight a defective gene," I said speculating, "you take a virus cell's first protein—the one that allows it to get into a human cell—and you replace the second protein with the protein that "fixes" the bad gene by creating its own gene type."

He smiled. "Yeah, that's about it."

"So what we need is the second protein."

"Yeah, and that's a simplification. We need to get the DNA structure of the defective gene and insert the second protein so that it fixes the problem but doesn't cause another problem. If it mutates into the wrong part of the gene, it could cause rapid multiplication of the gene—"he sighed, "We call that cancer."

"That's the big problem with gene therapy now?"

"Those are the big problems," he corrected. "Getting the right protein and getting it into the right spot."

"So this researcher, this Doctor Laird, the one who wrote the article about the orchid...maybe he found the protein?"

"That's the way I read it." He scratched his head. "That's a major step if that's the case."

"Man, we have to find him!" I wheeled my chair closer to the desk. "How can we find him, Steve?"

He shook his head. "My guess is that he's still in Hawaii. I've sent E-mails to just about every publication I can think of in the medical field." He grinned. "Yeah, I've been working on this one!"

I reached over the desk and clasped hands with him. "Thank you," I said fervently. "Thank you!"

We had lunch together and later that night I told Lindsey the good news. Both of us decided to brush up on gene therapy.

⊹⊱✶⊰⊹⊱✶⊰⊹

Some idiots are born that way, others grow up learning to be idiots from the people around them and some just choose to be stupid. That is the case with Frank Thornton. Frank was the idiot who shoved my wheelchair into Lindsey at the prom nearly rupturing her spleen. Thankfully, her spleen was able to recover on its own.

I kept it touch with Chuck because Lindsey just would not talk about her problems if she thought she could handle it. It was the one trait I sometimes wished she did not have. I wanted her to talk about her problems so I could get to know her better. Chuck did not hesitate to tell me shortly after the senior year began that Frank was acting all apologetic following Lindsey around. Chuck was convinced it was an act. Frank was hitting on Lindsey, he said.

I asked Lindsey about it one night. She studied me to gauge my reaction. "Right now he's just a nuisance. I told him to back off, leave me alone, all the stuff they teach you in sexual harassment courses." She grinned. "He's just being a pest. I think he feels bad about what he did."

I frowned, not satisfied with the wait-and-see attitude she prescribed. She said quickly, "Hey, there's nothing that you can do. Don't worry about it." She gave me that innocent, sweet girl look and added, "He doesn't really want to unleash the tiger inside this body, now, does he?"

My grin was from experience. "No, that's the truth."

"You know his parents took him out of school last year after it happened."

I knew that because Chuck told me. I was glad. Now I was worried. He might have a grudge against her or a vendetta. "So does he seem to be hitting on you because he likes you or because he wants to irritate you?"

She shrugged. "Who knows; anyway, I don't think he'll try anything stupid."

We talked for a while about gene therapy before Lindsey went home.

The next day in school, as if our discussion had created it, Frank caught Lindsey in the hallway. He fell into step beside her on her way to gym class. "Are you still seeing the cripple?"

"His name is Jimmy," Lindsey said, not reacting to Frank's barbed comment. She grinned, "I didn't realize he was a cripple!" She pretended to be shocked at the revelation.

Frank could not think of a comeback. He finally dropped off when Lindsey caught up to Cindy Hall, the girl who had been Chuck's date during the prom. She had become very good friends with Lindsey. "He's a jerk," Cindy told her. "Just ignore him."

They changed into gym shorts.

"Did you know he got arrested after his parents took him out of school?" Cindy continued.

"You mean thrown into jail, arrested?"

"Yup. He stole a car. That's the real reason he was out all last year. He's going to repeat his junior year this year." Cindy gave Lindsey a malicious grin. "Guess who reported it anonymously?"

Lindsey just stared at her friend.

"Yup, me and Chuck; we saw it!"

"Get out of here!"

Cindy leaned over and whispered in Lindsey's ear. "We were driving around, me and Chuck, looking for a place to park...and we saw someone trying to jimmy a car window. Chuck recognized Frank and he called 911 on his cell phone. He actually thought Frank was trying to get into his own car and did it to get back at him for what he did to you. But the car wasn't Frank's it turned out. So he has a rap sheet now."

"No wonder he's mad all the time," Lindsey replied.

When gym class was over Lindsey headed to the library. She had permission to take her study halls in the library as long as she wrote a two-page report on some topic she researched. She was having her usual trouble: cutting her reports to fit the teacher's expectations of what the rest of the class was capable of doing!

The library was across campus from the gym. Cindy walked with her part way and then went to her biology class. Lindsey's attention snapped back to the present when someone stepped into her path.

She stopped abruptly to avoid running into the person. Frank stood grinning at her. "I asked you a question and you ignored me." He looked around. The bell had rung for classes and there was nobody around. "Are you still seeing the cripple?"

"Are you sure he's a cripple?" Lindsey pretended to be shocked again.

Frank was once more at a loss for words.

"You better go now," Lindsey said gently. She stepped off the sidewalk to go around him, but he grabbed her arm. She pulled away but he wrapped his arms around her and held her.

"Frank! Let me go!" Lindsey was suddenly frightened.

Frank had her so tightly she could not turn and put a knee in his groin. She briefly considered kicking him but could not figure out how to get into the right position.

"Help!" Lindsey screamed suddenly and so loudly, that Frank let go and took a step back. Lindsey used the opportunity to run to the Library. She reported the incident to the librarian who immediately called security.

When she told me about it that night, I had to peel my fingers off the armrest of my wheelchair. For the first time in my life, I wished for a gun. I was not mad at Lindsey, she did the right thing, but I took it out on her because I felt so helpless.

"Damn it!" I said in frustration. "Why are there so many idiots?"

Lindsey watched me rant and rave for a few minutes. When I calmed down, she touched my arm to say something. I shook her hand off me and glared at her. The heat inside me was composed of frustration, fear, helplessness and a mix of other emotions I could not name. Once again, I could not protect her!

She waited patiently. She had frowned briefly when I shook her hand off. I raged at Frank for another minute and then saw her expression. The steam left me instantly.

"I'm sorry, Lindsey."

"I said I would handle it," she reminded me. "He's acting like an idiot, you're right about that. Idiots come to their own bad ends."

"Yeah," I acknowledged, "but sometimes they bring innocent people down with them."

She nodded. "The police and the principal know about it so I think I should be safe enough."

"I just wish I was there with you!"

"I've got plenty of people watching out for me," she said calmly.

"I feel so damn helpless!" I stared at her in frustration.

She waited.

"Have you told your parents?"

She nodded. "He accosted me. They're pressing charges."

I looked at her. She must be really frightened to allow that. "What charges?"

"Attempted kidnapping, assault and something else, I'm not sure."

"What about his friends—you know, Harold and Mark?"

She considered that. "I think Mark still hangs with him but Harold doesn't. I'm not sure why. Rumor has it that his dad threatened to emasculate him if he ever took another drink of alcohol, smoked a reefer or got in trouble. I think Harold took that seriously."

"That's what someone needs to do to Frank."

The tension in the room was the kind that had a hard time dissipating. Even after Lindsey left that night, I could not get rid of the anger in my heart. My whole body hurt with it. It affected the way she kissed me goodnight and the way I kissed her. It was the first kiss that seemed to originate and end at the lips.

Chapter 12

Lindsey was chess club president again her senior year and she was knocking down the competition. Our little rural school had developed a reputation. The Andersons began going to the chess matches. Before they watched Lindsey beat the prodigy her first year, they thought chess was equivalent to watching grass grow. But with Lindsey's success and reputation, chess matches had become as exciting as football at our little school. Home games drew crowds of sixty to seventy kids and adults. The matches moved to the cafeteria to accommodate the onlookers.

Chuck was vice president of the club. They did not face serious competition in any of the 2A School matches that year. However, Lindsey was more excited about the improvement of other members of the club who began to win more matches than they lost. That was something I had not accomplished as president.

This year the 3A match moved to our school. The 3A boys were determined to win back their school's prestige and trophy and this year's club was the best the school had ever had. So important was this contest that the principal of the 3A School vowed to show up at the tournament and asked the student body to turn out in support as well.

When the match began, the cafeteria quickly filled to overflowing with onlookers. I had a front row seat thanks to the wheelchair. Seated next to me was the principle of the 3A School. He introduced himself as Cletus Jones. We shook hands. "I think you were a past president, weren't you?" He asked after hearing my name.

"Yes, sir," I admitted.

I watched Lindsey play with confidence and poise. She never lost control of the board. The kids she played approached her with awe and fear. She won most of the games before she moved the first pawn. Her opponents were simply too nervous to concentrate on the game.

"I've played some," Mr. Jones said to me after watching Lindsey play for a while. "The brown-haired girl, Lindsey, is really good. How well do you know her?"

"A little," I said cautiously.

"Enough to introduce me after the match?" he asked.

"I don't know you that well," I said with a grin. After sitting in the exam room with a doctor a half dozen times this year I'd lost my fear of people. Everyone was a scared boy or girl somewhere down deep.

He appreciated the comment. "I'd like to invite her to enter a chess championship in New York."

"Why?" I was curious.

"She's beaten everyone she played in three years," he said with a lopsided grin. Then, tongue-in-cheek he added, "In case you didn't know." He did not know about the one match she lost and I was not going to enlighten him!

"I'm pretty sure she'd go if someone came up with the money."

He did not blink an eye. "Well, we can certainly discuss that."

Cletus Jones' name did not ring any bells with me. I tried hard to come up with his name. He said he had played some and it sounded like he played for more than just pleasure.

When Lindsey and Chuck swept the competition, the place went wild! Lindsey's first act was to shake hands with her final opponent, and then she came over to me and planted a kiss on my cheek.

The 3A School principal looked at me again. "You know her a little?" He grinned.

I said, "Lindsey, this is the principal of Placerville High School, Cletus Jones. He wants to invite you to a tournament in New York."

Lindsey shook hands with the balding, rather rotund principal. "Maybe you should meet my parents," she said. He nodded eagerly and walked with her to where her mom and dad were standing. I could see them talking for a minute before the crowd around Lindsey dragged her away from her parents. The principal stayed with the Andersons and they talked at length.

Eventually, Lindsey made it back to where I was waiting. "Quite a spectator sport now, thanks to you," I said.

She sat down and groaned. "My hand hurts!" She flexed her fingers. "I could never make it in politics!"

I pointed to the principal who remained chatting with her parents. "This guy seems pretty serious about getting you to that tournament."

"I'm game," she said. "But only if you can go."

Lindsey's parents seemed to like the idea and Mr. Jones. Apparently, he was somewhat famous even though we did not know him or his reputation. That night Lindsey had to stay home with her family so they could talk about it. It was not until the next day that she related the events to me. In the meantime I typed the principal's name into Google and found a dozen articles dated five years earlier—about the time Lindsey moved in next door.

The next day, Lindsey repeated what she knew. "Apparently Mr. Jones has some relationship with the chess tournament in New York. Every year he has entered his Chess Club members in it and the best they've ever done is made it to the second round."

I held my information back to let her talk.

"He told my parents that it didn't matter about the school because it wasn't school sponsored. He wanted to ask me last year but didn't—can you guess why?"

I could not.

"Remember that one game I lost when my parents were fighting me about coming over here?"

I nodded, remembering that awful time.

"He was at that match and wasn't impressed!" She giggled.

I laughed with her, appreciating the irony as much as she did. I guess he did know, after all.

"You're going to have to study up, buster," she said. "I need some real competition between now and April!"

"I'm your man," I said. "Let me tell you about Mr. Cletus Jones." I could barely contain the excitement that ran through me. "He played against one of the greatest chess masters ever!" I hunched forward. "He fought William Tallish, the Irish tournament champion, to a draw. He lost but he is famous because they drew six times in that tournament. If Mr. Jones would have won, he'd have walked away with a purse of $100,000."

Lindsey looked impressed.

"He gave up chess five years ago. At least, I guess he did. I haven't found anything about him after that in my research."

"That makes sense then," Lindsey mused. "He told my step dad that he was one of the organizers of the chess tournament in New York. He said he was going to look into getting a scholarship for me to go." Her eyes shone.

I took Lindsey to school each morning as usual even though I only went to the University on Monday, Wednesday and Thursday. I hated dropping her off and then driving away. She rode home with Cindy or another friend on the three days I was at school or when I had to meet with Steve Singleton. Cindy had a sweet little Mustang her parents bought her and she was a good driver so I felt okay about it. Funny how possessive I was feeling these days—or maybe protective is a better word.

Lindsey and I talked about me spending more time with her folks. I began making it a point to spend time in her house when we came home. It gave me a chance to talk to her mom and after a month or so, I began to feel better about our relationship. When her step dad got home though, I could feel the tension mount so I usually excused myself and went home.

I wished there was something that I could do with her step dad that would bond us. Playing golf was out of the question and he apparently loved to play. He had a regular golf match a couple times a month. I watched a few weekend tournaments on the television so I knew who the good players were in case we ever talked about golf but it never came up. I guess he didn't want to bring up a topic he figured I had no interest in and I didn't bring it up because he didn't. Stupid, I know.

My parents stumbled across a domino type game called Spinner that was fun to play. When Lindsey came over we sometimes played a game in the kitchen before going up to do our homework or talk. I loved the interaction between my parents and Lindsey. My mom and dad really loved her and she knew it. She often told me how good she felt with my mom. Occasionally I reminded her of the awesome belch she did not knowing my mom was around. I loved it when she blushed!

Lindsey finally suggested that we take the game of Spinner over to her house and see if her mom and dad would play it. I was dubious because they were not board game players. It would also mean a monumental shift in their attitude toward me; at least, that is what I thought.

Lindsey made the offer to her parents and to my surprise and hers, they accepted without hesitation. I hoped it would not turn into something other than a friendly get together when I rolled across the yard to her house that night. Her mom made tea and snacks and we took first ten minutes to explain the game and play one hand. They caught on and we started to play.

The game was fun and Lindsey won by thirty points. The lowest score was the winner because it meant you were not caught with high numbers in your hand when someone played their last cube.

Lindsey's mom suggested we retire the game and have cake and ice cream. I found her step dad unusually pleasant. I could tell Lindsey was encouraged by what she was feeling and she squeezed my shoulder as a signal that I was being a good boy.

"How are you feeling, Jimmy?" Her step dad asked when everyone settled in to eat cake and ice cream.

My suspicion was that this was an opening gambit for a discussion they wanted to have with us and I could feel my hands shaking slightly so I put them in my lap while I answered. "I'm feeling okay. My backside feels like ants are constantly crawling up and down on their way somewhere. I just wish they'd get there!"

Her mom suppressed a giggle. "Sorry, Jimmy. You just describe things in very picturesque terms."

Mr. Anderson glanced at his wife. "So, you're a junior in college. How do you like it?"

Now Lindsey was suddenly nervous. It did not help my stomach any. "I like it. I'm in a pre-med program but I'm

not planning to be a doctor. I want to do medical research."
I went on to explain about my mentorship and some of the
research I was doing on my own. I fell short of mentioning
Meckler's Disease when I got Lindsey's warning glance.

"Medical research," that is interesting. "What made you
decide on that field?"

I blushed and then said, "That time I got the blood
clot. I decided to see if I could help other paraplegics..." I
finished lamely.

"A very noble cause," Mr. Anderson said. I thought it
might be a trifle condescending but I was not sure.

The conversation rather petered out at that point. I
thought it was going somewhere but that might have been
my imagination. I was honestly relieved and I do not know
why.

We played six more times with the Andersons during
that month. I felt much more comfortable with them but
I could feel something unsaid. I wondered when it would
come out and if I would be ready for it. But then again,
maybe it was my imagination.

✦⋆✦⋆✦

The police came to school and interviewed Lindsey a
week after Frank Thornton had accosted her on the way
to the Library. They interviewed her in the Principal's
office. She learned during the interview that Frank had
fled the school immediately after the incident and that the
detectives were looking for him. That worried her but she
did not let me know until the next day as I was driving her
to school.

"Keep your eye out for Frank Thornton," Lindsey said
when we were about halfway to the school. I was enjoying
the day, happy about my blossoming relationship with her

parents—because that would only help when I asked if Lindsey and I could get married.

"What do you mean?"

"The police asked me about the incident again yesterday at school. I guess they are looking for him for some reason. They wouldn't tell me why, of course, except that he was wanted for something worse than truancy." I could see the look in her eyes had shifted to worry. It altered my attitude.

"Maybe because your parents filed charges?" I suggested.

She looked at me. Something else was bothering her.

"Lindsey, I don't want to go to school now," I said and pulled over to a safe area and stopped the car. "Damn! I wish Frank would just go away!"

"I know." She sat silent, watching me. Then she put a hand on my arm. "I'm not going to worry about it. I cannot let him control my happiness. Whatever happens do you remember what you said to me once?"

I shook my head. I had no idea where she was going with that.

"Someone might just be guiding us?"

I was astonished. Lindsey, the girl who only talked with certainty about things she had researched was speaking in religious terms!

"Don't look at me like that," she grinned. "I think higher thoughts sometimes. Do you remember when you were in the hospital? I went to the chapel to try to figure out how to deal with you..."

That was an understatement! She always thought higher thoughts, if you asked me. I felt at peace suddenly. I started the car and pulled back onto the highway. All the way to school that morning, I just kept looking at her. She was no longer worried. She was the confident, beautiful Lindsey.

Because of her confidence, I did not think about Frank all day. School occupied my attention and then therapy. After that, I had to meet with Steve for a mentoring session so when my phone buzzed at 4:30 that afternoon and I heard Lindsey's voice I was amazed at how fast the day had gone.

After greeting me, she said, "I just want you to know that I'm okay." My heart lurched. I was wheeling across the parking lot at Steve's office getting ready to leave. I pulled up beside my car and sat there with the warmth of the sun beating on my head. Sweat beads were forming on my body. "They caught Frank," she said when I did not respond because my heart was in my throat and I could not.

I could feel sweat trickling down my back and my legs felt funny, unusually funny but I ignored it. "What happened, Lindsey?" My voice was dry.

"I'll tell you when you get home. I just didn't want you to worry, that's all."

"Gee thanks! Now I'm worried. Lindsey, I can't drive home! What happened?"

"I can't really talk right now. I'm still at the police station."

I felt like throwing up. "Was it Frank?" I asked feeling weak.

"Yes, but everything's okay."

I wanted to keep her on the phone while I drove home but I could not. I reluctantly closed the phone and put it in my pocket. I was in a nervous sweat by the time I got my wheelchair loaded onto the seat next to me and drove out of the parking lot. It would take me almost an hour to get home and it was going to be the longest hour of my life!

I flipped the radio to the news channel. After twenty minutes of commercials — it seemed like — and ten minutes of Rush Limbaugh — the top of the hour news came on.

> *"A high speed chase ended peacefully a few hours ago when a Cross-field High School student surrendered to police and released his female hostage, another student at the high school. We'll have more details as they become available. The names of the suspect and his victim who are minors are being withheld by the Police."*

I had to pull over. I felt like I was going to be dizzy. Cars whizzed past me at a thousand miles an hour while I tried to focus enough to drive home. When I arrived, Lindsey's driveway was full of cars, reporters, and news cameras. I pulled in to my garage and shut the overhead door before I got out of the car.

Lindsey was in the kitchen talking to my parents. Her parents were looking out the window at the circus across the yard. "We came the back way," Lindsey said throwing her arms around me and hugging me. I held her so tight I thought she was going to protest but she did not. When I let her go, I begged her to tell me what happened.

Lindsey's parents and my parents had heard the story already but they listened with interest again. "At lunch I went to the library with Cindy. We kind of stick together since Frank did what he did a few weeks ago." She glanced at me. When I nodded to show that I remembered he had accosted her by the library, she continued. "He parked his dad's car in the parking lot just on the other side of the bushes that line the sidewalk. When Cindy and I walked by, he jumped out of the bushes, knocked Cindy down, and then grabbed me and threw me into the backseat. I was stunned because it happened so quickly."

Lindsey stopped to take a breath. "I didn't even know it was Frank until I started to sit up to get out of the car. He jumped into the driver's seat and put a gun in my face. 'Get on the floor or I'll blow your head off!' he said. All I could see was a great big hole at first. He was slobbering and trembling and I could see his finger tightening on the trigger so I just did what he said."

Tears gushed and we had to wait. Her mom moved over, sat by her on the couch, and put her arms around her. After a minute she continued. "The car was a station wagon. He was so nervous he sideswiped a car and broke the glass. I felt it landing on my feet. I wanted to jump out and run but he didn't even look, he just accelerated out of the parking lot and into traffic. I bet we were doing thirty miles an hour by the time we reached the street!"

I could not stop trembling as I listened. I think her step dad saw that I was about to have a nervous breakdown and did something I will never forget. He got up, came over to where I was, and put a hand on my shoulder. Then he just stood there listening to the rest of Lindsey's story.

Cindy called the police. Frank had knocked her down when he grabbed Lindsey so she would not interfere. While he was squealing out of the parking lot with Lindsey in the back seat, Cindy was talking to the 911 operator. Within thirty seconds, she saw a police car speeding past the school. A few seconds later, every police car in town was screaming toward the freeway in hot pursuit.

"I kept my head down and prayed," Lindsey said. The car swayed like a boat and I got as small as I could get on the floor. I had no idea what he was going to do. I prayed that he wouldn't commit suicide." She smiled through her tears. "I suddenly felt calm. I sat up and began to talk to him. He was scared. The cops were everywhere. I said, 'Frank, thanks for the ride, but you're going in the wrong direction. I live on the other side of town.' I could see the speedometer was eighty miles an hour."

Lindsey paused for a breath and a drink. "He just started to cry. He slowed down and pulled over and put his hands out the window crying."

Mr. Anderson squeezed my shoulder. "We spent most of the afternoon at the police station. I don't think Frank is going to be bothering Lindsey anymore."

My mom offered drinks around and cookies. When Mrs. Anderson got up to help her, I took Lindsey's hands. She looked at me. "I felt so calm, Jimmy. Remember what I said to you on the way to school?"

I nodded, tears leaking.

"It was as if a big arm just came down and went around my shoulders. I felt safe. I knew what to say. I meant it to be light-hearted and joking. When he broke down, cried, and pulled over I could not believe it. It didn't last more than fifteen minutes."

When interviewed by the detectives, Frank said he did not want to hurt her. He had become the butt of jokes because Lindsey preferred someone in a wheelchair to him. He knew that Lindsey went to the Library at that time each day so he decided to talk some sense into her. He was sure she would not listen to him because he had already blown it with her so the only thing left was to make her listen to him. To do that, he had to get her away from her friends. He claimed he was in a mental fog until Lindsey's calm words that he was going the wrong direction snapped him out of it. The double meaning hit him and made him realize that his whole life was heading the wrong direction. That is when he broke down and surrendered.

After Lindsey and her parents snuck out the back door and went home, my mom and dad sat in the living room with me. "She's one of the bravest people I know," my dad said. He gave me an approving look. "She's always been that way."

My dad did not say much but when he did, it was right to the point.

Mom smiled.

That night I lay in bed looking at the ceiling. "Thank you," I said into the darkness. "Whoever you are, thanks."

⊢⊣⊢⊣⊢⊣⊢

Dr. Steve Singleton called with some exciting news. He had gotten a response to one of his hundred e-mails. The response was from a relative of Dr. Jeremiah Laird, the researcher who had written the Cataleya Orchid report. The relative was a brother who promised to do what he could to help. He told Steve that he had not heard from his brother in three months but that was not unusual. He was in Hawaii or at one of the islands doing research. Then he told Steve that their father had died of Meckler's Disease.

Steve called me right away. While he was talking, I suddenly remembered something that happened to me. I had noticed it while Lindsey was talking to me on the day of the kidnapping while I was in his parking lot.

"Steve, remember the day Lindsey was kidnapped?"

"Yeah."

"My legs felt weird," I said.

He paused and then said dryly, "Describe *weird*."

"I felt pressure on my legs."

Steve got excited. "I want to see you right away!" He shouted it into the phone. "How soon can you get here?"

"Steve, it's been a week. Let me wait until our next mentoring session Tuesday," I begged.

"Okay, okay. I don't have time today anyway." He made me promise to come on Tuesday. I had never missed an appointment so his concern was excitement more than anything else.

On Tuesday, I did not have classes at the University so we met at 9:00 in the morning. He was waiting impatiently. "I've got to test you!" He said. He led me into the exam room. He squeezed my leg just above the knee—the same place my dad used to when I was a kid. He always made me squirm because it hurt.

"Can you feel this?" Steve asked.

"When you squeeze hard, yes," I said quietly and in shock. I'd been afraid to tempt fate by testing it myself.

Steve tried a few other places lower down on my leg. I felt the pressure each time. "It's really happening, Jimmy," he said softly. "It's really happening."

I could not wait to tell Lindsey.

That night I told Lindsey what was happening in my legs and we talked until 10:00 p.m. before Lindsey noticed the time. She kissed me goodbye and dashed out the door. I hoped it would not hurt the new better relationship with her parents. I got ready for bed and lay there for a while thinking about what it could mean. My parents were excited. She was going to tell her parents. I felt happy.

I woke up around midnight with spasms in my legs. It was so painful I hit the intercom button and called my mom and dad. I felt just like I'd cramped up playing football! My mom and dad had no idea what to do so they called Steve who called Dr. Lang and woke him up in South America. By the time he called us back the spasms had subsided.

"You can expect that to happen more frequently, Jimmy," "he warned me. "As the nerves begin to do their job, they see stuff that is not right and try to fix it. The only thing you can do is wait it out. It shouldn't last more than ten minutes."

"But what is it? What's causing that to happen?" I asked.

"It sounds like the nerves are arcing. They're growing, Jimmy! If they get too close together, they short out and your muscles cramp up. I think we talked about this before the surgery."

After I hung up, my mom and dad stared at me. "Well?" Mom said.

I told them what the doctor said and then complained, "I never knew how long ten minutes could last!"

"Try having a baby," my mom said somewhat unsympathetically.

"What do I do if I'm driving and this happens?"

"For the next three months, you better let someone else drive," Steve said. "That's how long Dr. Lang said this might last."

"Is there anything I can do?" I wanted to know.

"Exercise, buddy, exercise," Steve said cheerfully. "You gotta pay the price. Didn't football teach you that?"

I threw myself into exercising with a passion. I wanted to keep the cramps and my agony from Lindsey—call it a perverse need to surprise her with my progress. I wanted to surprise her by standing up from my wheel chair and holding her in my arms. I was determined to do that as soon as possible.

My mom began to drive me to the university. Lindsey was concerned, scared, worried that I was not driving but I told her it was because my car was out of commission and needed to be fixed. She accepted that because I never lied to her. I worried about that. I hoped it would not come back to haunt me in a big way. Nevertheless, I was determined not to let her know about the cramps.

They came at night. Great, massive bolts of pain out of the blue would grip me and twist me until I was sweaty and sobbing. I never called my parents after that first time. I buried my face in my pillow and waited for the torture to ease. The worst thing about any pain is the unknown. Once you know what is going on, it's easier to face. The cramps began to come regularly almost every night as if some malevolent force had me pinned down and delighted in torturing me! Fortunately, they only hit once a night, no more.

I remembered Dr. Lang's words about some patients only getting this far in their recovery and I thought—if that happens to me, I'll take a gun to myself. The only thing that kept me sane was the hope that there would come a day when these muscle-wrenching cramps would end.

During March, and right up until the tournament in April, Lindsey and I played over a hundred games of chess in preparation for New York. Lindsey wanted to have Principal Jones tutor her in chess but her parents nixed that idea. She did the second best thing and played a few games with him via e-mail at the end of March. She lost but Dr. Jones was encouraging in that he said she was very good. He gave her some pointers before he hung up.

Lindsey put his advice to immediate use. She asked me to play specific combinations of moves against her from games played by the masters. She did not want to know what particular game or master I chose so that she could get a feel for the tournament conditions. I chose some obscure masters from two centuries ago and studied their moves. I pitted them against Lindsey repeatedly, in different combinations, until she recognized the plays and found a defense against them. Soon she was recognizing them within two or three moves and countering easily. I suggested she play Dr. Jones again and she challenged him that night a week before the tournament.

This time Lindsey countered every move he made. He called and continued the game over the phone. The game ended in a draw. He told Lindsey she was more prepared than anyone he had ever tutored.

The chess tournament took place in late April over a weekend. We flew to New York separately. Her family had an anonymous sponsor who funded their trip. We never knew who, but I suspected Steve Singleton was behind it in some way.

We did not realize that Lindsey would be the star attraction at the chess tournament. It was a lot of pressure on her and she held up well the first day but her nature was one that fled from the limelight. Match play began on day two. When Lindsey wasn't playing, she was barraged by questions. They all wanted to know how it felt to be a girl player at this level, if she was going to win and so on. Dr. Jones smiled with pride as he anticipated Lindsey taking the chess world by storm.

The tournament was age-based so Lindsey was in the 17 to 18-year-old division. There were no other females in the competition and the boys were mostly of Asian or Indian heritage. Here and there were a few Caucasians and blacks, but no other females to take the attention of the media off Lindsey.

She faltered right away in her first chess match. With cameras and flashbulbs popping and snapping every time she moved a chess piece, she began to doublethink every move. The boy across from her had been there before. He expected to win and he was good. Lindsey lost in thirty-two moves.

It was a double elimination tournament, which meant that Lindsey had lost once and she would be out of the match if she lost twice. Her next opponent was a very skilled player who was last year's champion. Before the match, Lindsey came and sat down next to me.

"I didn't do very well," she said. "I couldn't think."

"There are too many people who will be disappointed if you don't win, right?"

She nodded miserably.

"Then I guess you just have to play as if today is the last time you will pick up a pawn. Maybe tomorrow all of your fingers fall off. Who knows, it could happen." I held her hand and moved each digit. "Yeah, I think this one's ready to fall." I wiggled her pinky.

She grinned and gave me the look. "I'm being pretty stupid to worry about what these guys think of me, right?"

"I think you're pretty great. Who cares what they think."

She held my hand tightly for a second or two and then got up. "Do you think I can win?"

I shook my head affirmatively.

"Then that's what I'll do."

When she sat down, I knew the other boy was in trouble because she began to play with a ringlet by her ear. When she twisted her hair with two fingers, she was concentrating. She recognized his King's Gambit opening and let it play out until she was able to counteract it with one of Serchez's moves. He apparently had not seen that because he fell into the trap and in six more moves she called checkmate.

Lindsey drew white on the next game and she opened with Fray's Attack. The boy across from her failed to recognize the danger and countered with standard moves that should have been good with any other opponent. Lindsey beat him and suddenly the crowds around her table began to grow again.

Lindsey won the next two matches and the tournament paused for lunch. After two hours, it resumed and Lindsey won the afternoon matches. By the end of the day, only four people remained and Lindsey was one of them. The chess match would resume at 10:00 a.m.

That night Lindsey and I went to the observation lounge in the Hotel. It was quiet and the view of New York's lights was amazing. It was nice to look down on the Big Apple and not see the wormholes. The lights were beautiful. The night was clear and cloudless and the lounge was dark. We talked about the tournament for a little while and then turned our thoughts to more important things.

"I've had a good life, Jimmy," Lindsey said. We were holding hands in a dark part of the lounge. There were not very many people around us.

I looked at her. Her fingers were squeezing mine as if an electrical pulse was running through her. "It's a good life so far," I corrected her.

"No, I mean it. Look at all the things I've been blessed with," she said fervently. "I have you, my parents, I'm going to be valedictorian, like you were, and I have lots of friends..."

"Lindsey, what are you trying to say?" I did not like the direction the conversation was taking.

"Maybe I'm having second thoughts about my optimism. Everyone says I'm too optimistic."

"Not me," I corrected her again.

"I know, not you, Jimmy. But a lot of the teachers at school think I'm looking at life as I want it to be instead of as it really is."

I sat silently. Her fingers pulsed.

"They say it's a mistake to be excessively optimistic. Like some of the great philosophers of the past: Niche, Kierkegaard...others," Her voice trailed off.

"Lindsey," I spoke at last, hoping I understood enough to talk about it. "You are not excessively optimistic. You are a realist with an abundance of hope. I've seen you hope for the best in every situation while observing the thing as it really was."

"Maybe I'm just scared," she admitted.

"Of what, exactly?" I asked.

"I think it's the realist in me that says Meckler's disease is going to win. There's too much stacked against beating it."

"How can you say that? We don't understand enough to know what the odds are."

"Everyone who dies — dies young." She replied quietly.

We looked out the window. After a few minutes, I pressed her hand. "Are you worried about tomorrow?"

"Not tomorrow — tomorrow," she said, "but the future, yeah, I feel a little worried."

I waited.

"I didn't worry until you started getting ants in your pants," she giggled at her own humor and it lightened the mood briefly. When she sobered, she said, "I began to think that maybe you would get better and Romeo and Juliet would happen: I'd die." Lindsey suddenly burst into tears.

I was shocked. Rarely had Lindsey admitted to doubts or fears since I had known her. I leaned over and pulled her onto my lap. I put my arms around her and held her while she cried quietly in the empty room. When at last her tears subsided, she wiped them away with a napkin.

"You've been my strength, Lindsey," I said resting my chin lightly on her shoulder. "You have carried me through the most difficult times of my life. But, Lindsey, nobody can do that for as many people for as long as you have without getting tired."

I kissed her cheek lightly. "I'm going to be your strength tonight. Can you feel the strength in my arms?" I held her tightly. "Can you feel the strength of my heart beating right next to yours? That is where it will be all the days of our lives. After tonight, Lindsey, we are going to go out into this world and finish what we have started. We will not quit. I won't and you won't."

We sat in silence for a long time just being together. When at last someone entered the lounge, Lindsey stirred and got off my lap. The person walked back out, not seeing anyone else. Lindsey knelt beside me and put her head on my lap. "I'll let you be my strength, Jimmy."

I stroked her hair. "You know what you taught me that day when we talked to your mom and dad, Lindsey?"

"No," she looked at me.

"That you should always live until you die." I grinned at her.

Her fingers reflected that her spirit was calming down. The pulse stopped. "There really isn't anything I can do about Meckler's disease, is there?" She asked.

"Not a single thing," I agreed.

"In that case, I'm going to live until I die!" Then she kissed me.

The next morning Lindsey won the first match. The crowd erupted in applause as she called checkmate and sat back in her chair. Her opponent wiped the sweat off his brow with the handkerchief he had been using regularly, and then admitted to defeat. He shook hands with her and walked away.

Lindsey now faced the one person that had defeated her. He was confident and had the advantage of starting the game. Someone next to me whispered that Lee Young was the best young chess player they had ever seen. I looked over at Principal Jones and saw his look of anticipation. He had never made it this far with any of his players before. Already he seemed to be thrilled. Lindsey had made it to the final round!

Lindsey's face was blank. She would wait for the first move and then her features would wind up like a clock under tension. I knew how that wonderful mind worked. The thing that bothered me was her hand. She was not touching her hair. Then she glanced over at me and smiled. I felt relief wash through me. It would be okay.

Lee Young's opening move silenced the anticipatory murmurs in the audience; it was the standard King's-pawn-four. Lindsey countered and the game was on. Move after move the two of them fought for control of the center four squares. Lee was squeezing Lindsey out of the squares and she would recover. It was fitting that the last match of the tournament would come down to the most basic moves.

Lee moved his King's Bishop out and Lindsey countered. He moved his King's Knight out and Lindsey countered. I could see that he was playing with more than just confidence. He was playing carelessly. I understood immediately that he considered Lindsey lucky, not skilled. I sat back and could not help but grin. Lindsey took advantage of Lee's carelessness and pride. She hesitated over a couple of moves and drew Lee's attention to those moves. I saw her do it and understood that she was leading him to make a decision based on her feints.

There comes a moment when you realize you have been had. Lee's face fell when he realized that moment. Lindsey had him and he knew it. He valiantly played the game to the end and then looked at his female opponent as if seeing her for the first time. It was a look of respect. I was glad Lindsey had taken advantage of the boy's carelessness and knew that he would not make that mistake again. Lindsey took no pride in the win, she merely put his king in checkmate and reached across the table and shook Lee's hand. The crowd erupted in applause.

Lee looked disconsolate. He had expected to sweep the tournament. It was his first loss and it bothered him because he had gotten careless, thinking Lindsey was not his equal.

Lindsey had white on the second game. She tested Lee by opening with Horatio's Attack. Lee knew that one and the game ended in a draw. Lee opened his next with Gioacchino Greco's standard opening. Lindsey countered it and the game turned into a draw. Both of them went back and forth using the great master's openings, testing each other.

The afternoon wore on with neither player showing the least signs of fatigue. The crowd sighed with each draw. Finally, Lindsey had White again and she opened with Fray's Advance. Lee seemed confused by the opening and missed countering it with the best move. Lindsey took advantage of it. She went on the attack and Lee found himself scrambling to cover. He managed to get his footing back when Lindsey made a single, small mistake. She recovered quickly and pressed the attack again. Both players struck repeatedly until it looked like a draw was inevitable. Lindsey had one pawn left and both bishops. Lee was down to his queen and king. The crowd was on the edge of their seats as Lindsey marched her pawn down each rank while trying to keep Lee from putting her in check and capturing the pawn. Lee was desperate. He would have to sacrifice his queen because Lindsey controlled the squares that the pawn was on with her bishops.

Incredibly, Lee managed to put Lindsey in check and capture one of her bishops without losing his queen but Lindsey countered by putting his king in check with her remaining bishop. He had to move his king, which allowed Lindsey then to advance to the final rank and regain her queen. Since she had forced him onto the last rank, he was in check the moment she regained her queen. He had to place his queen between Lindsey's queen and his king. Instead of taking his queen at the cost of her own and ending the game in another draw, Lindsey moved her queen and put Lee in check once more. He countered by moving his queen. Now Lindsey was in danger by Lee's queen if she moved her queen. She could not move it back to where she had previously had him in check because that would begin the countdown for a draw. She took a gamble and took Lee's queen with her own. Lee took Lindsey's queen with his king and now the race was on. Lee had to escape long enough to win a draw. Lindsey began to move in with her king and bishop.

The first move favored Lindsey because she was able to keep him pinned on the back rank with her bishop. Slowly and with carefully thought out movements, Lindsey managed to get him into the corner where she put him in checkmate.

The audience roared its approval. Lindsey was the first female ever to win the tournament previously dominated by men. She accepted her trophy and a full, four-year scholarship to the college of her choice. She walked quickly to where we were waiting and begged us to get her out of there. Cletus Jones came to us with shining eyes and hugged Lindsey. "I didn't recognize your gambit on that final match," he said. "But you were brilliant!"

Chapter 13

Steve told me he was going to fly to Hawaii in the summer. It was the first opportunity he had to take a vacation and he was going to use it to look for Dr. Laird.

My feet hurt like the devil all the time now. The fire spread into my calves and sometimes up the back of my leg making me itch like crazy. I scratched and rubbed when Lindsey was not around.

Lindsey had come into her own during her senior year. The thing with Frank could have devastated her but the feeling of calm and of being looked after, even in the middle of that, changed her. She was assured, mature, and kinder than ever before. I watched her interact with people. She was never one to take something wrong. She never complained. Some nights I just stared at her while she did homework. She clutched a pencil between her teeth and tangled a curl around her finger while she studied. She would catch me looking at her, give me a brilliant smile, and then go back to what she was doing. In a moment, she would raise her eyes to see if I was still watching and if I was—which was always—she would reach across the table and catch my hand. A little while later, it would start all over again.

One night I noticed that she was taller. *When did she grow up?* I asked myself. The way I measured it was her height in the doorway. I made marks, nearly invisible marks, with a pencil taped to a ruler. The highest I could reach with pencil and my arm from the wheelchair was five feet ten inches. The last time she came through the doorway she was five feet eight inches tall. She had youthful beauty the kind that comes from freshly stretched skin and an inner happiness. Even when she frowned, the effect was pleasing. Her brown, green-flecked eyes, her lips and hourglass figure— which she hid most of the time—made her an outwardly attractive girl. The depth of her soul, her kindness and her genuine joy at being with you and her interest in you made you realize that she was infinitely lovelier than could be discerned by a casual glance.

A pretty girl would catch my eye now and then— especially at college. But after five seconds of conversation with them, I knew that none of them was half the woman Lindsey was. Most of them had no idea where real beauty came from or what it was. They were trading on their outer beauty to get them through life. They were not kind unless it got them something; they were not helpful unless the spotlight was on them; and they were not wise. Some of them were smart with knowledge but they were not wise enough to listen to a child, hear an old woman, give a man respect or counsel a boy about girls. Most of them missed it because they were so concerned about how people viewed them that they could not see others. Most of them only pretended to be interested in others.

❧

Lindsey was easily the Valedictorian. Her grade point average never dropped below 4.0 the entire four years of High School. She took her SATs and scored 1560 the first time and 1570 the second time. It was not a perfect 1600, but it was in the top one percent.

She would not practice the speech in front of me. She wanted me to hear it for the first time when she gave it in front of the school on graduation night. I was anxious to hear what she had to say.

When she got up to give that valedictorian speech, I predicted there would not be a dry eye in the house. I also predicted that everyone would go out of that place richer for having been there.

On graduation night, I was a nervous wreck. I knew Lindsey would do very well but I was sweating bullets anyway. The gymnasium was packed and the air was hot already from all the bodies. I had a prime location, near the front of the gym on the floor. I would only be a dozen paces from Lindsey when she stood to give her speech. The school had arranged a platform for her to stand on so that everyone could see her.

When the moment came, I felt a shiver run up and down my back. I felt like chewing my fingernails and hiding at the same time. Instead, I reminded myself that I was going to be the strong one for Lindsey—just as I had promised in New York. I sat up straight, smiled and relaxed as much as I could. She could read tension in my body better than anyone could, and I wanted her to see me calm.

Lindsey had the single gold tassel and the pin. When the Principal announced her as the Valedictorian speaker, a hush ran through the audience. It was as if everyone had come just for this moment. She got up, walked quickly to the platform, and stepped up onto it. Her smile radiated through the gymnasium, lighting it. Her hair hung loosely over her shoulders and she appeared to be relaxed. I caught my breath as she glanced toward me.

"Everyone tells us that we are about to begin the great adventure of life. I don't agree. Everyone says that preparation time is over. Again, I don't agree.

They, the folks who profess to speak for high school graduates everywhere, say that the greatest days of our lives are ahead of us. But what makes that so?"

There was stunned silence and a slight twitter moved through the assembled students. Gray heads in the bleachers caught their collective breath and leaned forward.

"We are what we are today because we chose to be what we are. Nothing that you are has been thrust upon you—it was chosen by you. You became you because of how you met the hard times of your life. You became what you are by how you skated or persevered in the lazy or easy times of your life. You will be what you can be only if you rise to the challenge of becoming—not coasting. Benjamin Franklin's secret of success is your secret to a successful life—one that means something to you. Ben said, 'I never put off until tomorrow, the thing that I can do today.' That little saying is the motto a successful person's life. Never fail to study today or say hello to a hurting person or kiss your best friends' hurts today. Never fail to tell someone today that you appreciate them, love them, and cherish them. Never fail to see the good in someone when it is disguised by hurt, sorrow and fear. Never fail to meet the challenges of today, today. Pay your debts today. And most of all; live today as if you won't have tomorrow. That is what Ben Franklin meant."

Lindsey paused and looked over a quiet crowd.

"We are not about to begin the greatest adventure of our lives, my friends. We are in the greatest adventure. It started when you took your first breath and it may be over tomorrow for some of us. What if you don't

have tomorrow? Ben Franklin's words are sharply in focus. Never put off until tomorrow what you can do today.

"And what about preparation time; is it over? No. It is always going on. You are preparing to be tomorrow's person today. We are preparing to be moms, dads, and grandparents today and if we do not know that, we will be untrue to what we could have been. You and I have struggled for twelve years—some of us a little longer—..."

There was a rush of laughter and then quiet.

"...and we are today the result of those struggles. Each day we add preparation for the day beyond.
"Do not put off until tomorrow what can be done today."

With that, she sat down.

The audience knew Lindsey's character. She was the girl who helped others study. She was the girl who welcomed the new kids and did not react to the clique's barbs and jibes. She was the single girl to win the New York Invitational Chess Tournament. Now they rose to their feet as one person and clapped in one sustained roar.

Chapter 14

My first pain-free night since the cramps began happened in June. I was so relieved that I told my mom and dad about it at breakfast. I had lain awake all night waiting for the cramps to hit. Mom and dad checked the calendar. "It's early for that," mom said happily.

"I know. Everything seems to be speeding up." I was tired. "I think I'll take a nap before Lindsey comes over today."

I wanted to talk to my parents about Lindsey. Lindsey and I had talked about marriage and we were both in agreement that it would happen, but I still wanted to do some things the old-fashioned way. The first thing I had to do was ask my mom and dad for their blessings. I did that in the middle of June.

Mom and dad listened to me as I asked for their blessing. It was the first foray into the chancy territory of getting parental approval. I knew my parents were solidly behind me. That's why it was easier to start with them. It was the right place to start, no matter what.

I felt as if Lindsey's speech was meant for one person in that audience alone: me. She was telling me not to put off the hardest thing I would have to do—ever. I needed to talk to her parents about our desire to be married. I drew courage from her speech. I think the hundreds in the audience that night did too.

My mom and dad listened to me and then dad spoke. "Son, Lindsey is the finest girl two people could ever wish for in a daughter-in-law. She's already like a daughter to us."

He stopped. I could tell he was getting emotional or that he was struggling to control his emotions. "We certainly will give you two our blessing. You will never have a handicap when you marry her. And, I wish for you all the happiness that marriage has to offer."

My mom wiped tears from her eyes. "I don't know if I ever told you this in any of our talks," she said. "I came up the steps to the room...I think it was the first or second day Lindsey came to see you." Her eyes twinkled at the memory. "She burped just as I stepped into the room and you nearly fell on the floor because you laughed so hard. Jimmy, I never thought I would hear you laugh again!" Tears filled her eyes. "I fell in love with Lindsey then. Nothing— I mean it—nothing has changed my mind about her! She's honest, caring and devoted to you." She wiped her hands on her apron. "When I hear you talk about her, I'm thrilled."

She looked at me steadily for a moment and then smiled. "You asked me once if it was okay to love Lindsey...I haven't changed my mind, Jimmy." Again, she paused to swallow. "I love Lindsey. I love her. You marry her, Jimmy."

I wanted to get their advice about the Andersons but I knew what I had to do.

I dropped Lindsey off at the mall telling her that I needed to see someone about a very important proposal. She waved goodbye and blew me a kiss. Because I could not go with her, she was meeting Cindy.

I had made an appointment with her parents and asked them to keep it a secret from Lindsey. They agreed, thankfully. I drove back home with my speech and hopes rushing full throttle through my head.

Mrs. Anderson offered me a coke and I accepted gratefully. They sat down on the couch side by side and looked at me.

"Thank you for meeting with me," I said nervously. They smiled at my nervousness but said nothing. Encouraged a little, I continued. "I've loved your daughter by stages over the last five years. I wish I could tell you how it happened or why but I can't. When I was an angry, lost boy and she was just eleven years old, she opened the door to my heart and walked in. She knows my heart better than I do."

The Andersons looked at each other and then back at me. I took a sip of coke, hoping I would not choke on it. I had gone home and changed into my best clothes for this. I hoped the sweat that I felt on my upper lip was invisible to them.

"When you came home from vacation four years ago I teased her about her Boston accent. Before she left that day, she leaned down and kissed my cheek. It made me angry because of my handicap. A few years ago when we were at the beach house on vacation..." I had to wipe my eyes because I suddenly had trouble seeing and speaking. They waited for me to continue. Mrs. Anderson reached for a box of Kleenex and walked it over to me. I took one and wiped my eyes. "...while we were there, we sat on the front porch and Lindsey told me that she wanted me...to bring her back to this beach, to this house, for our honeymoon.

"Just after my blood clot, the last night at the hospital, I tried to drive her away. I was afraid that I would just cause her more grief if a blood clot broke loose and caused me to have a stroke or heart attack or killed me...but she was there when I woke up and told me in no uncertain terms never to do that again."

Mrs. Anderson smiled as she recognized Lindsey in my words.

"She didn't so much as tell me that she loved me as

remind me of that fact. She had been telling me in dozens of ways. I was just too wrapped up in myself to see it. She finally had to take my face in her hands and hold it while she told me." It was my turn to smile at the recollection.

I looked at them. I was surprised to see Mr. Anderson wiping his eyes with a Kleenex.

"She has never wavered in her belief in me. She has never once seen my wheelchair as a problem or a hindrance." I looked up again. "I'm here today to tell you that I know I could never, ever live up to her view of me, but I want your permission to spend the rest of my life trying. I want your permission to marry Lindsey."

I steeled myself for all the reasons why it would not work. I prepared my arguments for why it would work.

Mrs. Anderson spoke first. "Jimmy, it's a little early to be asking about marriage. Lindsey is only seventeen. She's pretty young to have her mind made up."

"Yes ma'am," I said. It was true.

Mrs. Anderson smiled at me. "You and Lindsey have talked about this, haven't you?"

"Just what I said earlier; she just assumed right off that I would agree with her about marriage. She told me when she was, um, thirteen that we were going to get married."

"She speaks her mind," Mrs. Anderson sighed. "What do you think about that, Jimmy?"

"About her telling me she was going to marry me?" I shook my head. "I told her we were too young to talk about marriage...I think I said 'it was weird.' She didn't get mad. She just said, 'I'm just telling you Jimmy Turner that I want to come here for our honeymoon.'" I grinned at the memory. Vacation on the beach seemed so long ago now.

"She is very mature for her age," Mr. Anderson said as if reminding himself and Lindsey's mom of that fact.

"Yes, sir, she is." I wiped a bit of sweat from my brow using the Kleenex Mrs. Anderson had given me earlier.

"But what do you think about her speaking her mind?" Mrs. Anderson clarified her question.

"I have come to appreciate that about her because she's never mean. She is blunt at times because most of us beat around the bush all our lives about things. She's as honest as anyone I've ever met." I looked at them earnestly. "Did I tell you about the time she accidentally broke a dish at our house?" They shook their heads. I told them about it. "When she told my mom, all my mom did was hug her for a long time. My mom and dad really love her."

There was a long pause then, "How will you provide for her?" It was Mr. Anderson's question.

"I'm going to graduate from college next year. I'll have a degree that will help me get into the field of medical research. My mentor, Dr. Singleton says he wants me on his staff as soon as possible after I graduate. I've already done some work for him and he likes it." I felt embarrassed to be bragging on myself.

"I'm sure you will be able to take care of her. You already know about her disease, don't you?"

I looked at Mr. Anderson stunned. I nodded, unable to speak.

"And you have been devoting a lot of time to researching Meckler's disease, haven't you?" Mr. Anderson said as his wife watched with tear-brimmed eyes.

"Yes sir. I'm going to devote my life to Lindsey," I said quietly.

Mrs. Anderson burst into tears and fled from the room. Mr. Anderson and I waited until she came back about five minutes later. She had drinks on a tray to cover up her sudden departure. Her eyes glittered as she gave me the coke. She clutched the remaining drink in her hand and impulsively leaned down and kissed my cheek. "Thank you, Jimmy."

When she sat back down, Mr. Anderson cleared his throat and looked at his wife. She nodded and cleared her throat, took a sip of coke and put the glass down carefully on the table. I figured out instantly that they had arranged their own speech or speeches for me and this was it. I steeled myself.

Mrs. Anderson went first. "I would be proud to have you as my son," she said. Her voice choked with emotion. "Lindsey would not even consider anyone else. You have had such an impact on her, Jimmy. If you two live up to just one one-millionth of your potential together, it will be more than most couples ever achieve." She got up and made her way to where I was. She leaned down and kissed my cheek again and then walked back to sit by her husband.

He cleared his throat. "You know that Lindsey is not my biological daughter, but I feel like she is my own. I'm going to speak for her biological dad, Jimmy. He would be proud of you for the way that you have changed in the last few years. I am too. When we found out that you were researching Meckler's disease to help Lindsey, and that you had abandoned your blood clot research, we could barely believe it. But we do believe it because we know what kind of a man you are now." He had to clear his throat a couple of times before he could continue. "I'm trying to say, Jimmy, that you have my blessings from the bottom of my heart." Again, he paused before continuing. "We know she's young in chronological age but in maturity, she might be older than all of us together. So you have our blessings Jimmy."

I could scarcely believe the reception and thanked my silent benefactor, whoever he or she was. I did not know who, but someone had provided information about my research to the Andersons. After we talked a little longer, I looked at my watch. Lindsey and I had agreed on a time for me to pick her up at the mall.

I had one more request for the Andersons. They happily agreed to it.

I changed clothes and returned to the mall at the appointed time. I told Lindsey that I would like to take her out for supper and I wanted to pick her up in the same way I did for the prom. I said, "I think my parents are going to be at your house for games or something tonight. We could stay if you want."

"No, it would be nice to go out tonight." She grinned at me. I knew she wanted to go out and guessed I was teasing her.

"Very formal," I told her.

"Okay," she looked at me. I could see her eyes twinkling with anticipation. Somehow, I had a reputation for being romantic and she loved being surprised. That is why she did not ask where we were going or why she had to dress up.

I told her when I would pick her up and she said she would be ready. She was never late.

I told my parents and they went over to the Andersons at 5:45 p.m. to play Spinner. They even set the table up with the Spinner game. I arrived at 5:55 and did not ring the doorbell. Mrs. Anderson opened the door, winked at me, and ushered me inside.

In two minutes, I was in position and waiting.

Lindsey came down the steps in a formal, full length, pink dress with beautiful earrings and necklace. Her hair was done up in ringlets because she knew I loved that. She floated down the steps and walked into the living room where her parents and my parents were at the table with the game of Spinner spread out in front of them. She did a double take. Both sets of parents were on the far side of the table, facing the living room. Lindsey noticed. She looked at them and then she noticed me.

I was wearing a Tux with matching black shoes. I was in a very unusual position. Lindsey's dad had helped me sit on a small footstool in front of a kitchen chair they had arranged next to me for this occasion. Both moms were trying hard to hold back tears. Lindsey looked at me puzzled. My legs were bent so that I was kneeling in front of the chair.

"I need to show you something," I said. I patted the seat of the empty chair next to me. She came over slowly and sat down. I could tell she was mystified by the arrangement. Suddenly comprehension flooded into her features. She looked at me. Her face turned pink nearly matching her dress. She looked at her mom who was already dabbing a Kleenex to her eyes in anticipation.

"Oh my," Lindsey said. Her hand fluttered to her face and then to her heart.

I took her hands and held them. "Lindsey Schnetler," I said, "I fell helplessly in love with you sometime in the last five years. You alone, of all people in this world, have my heart in your hands. You mean more to me than life itself. I want to share your life and I want you to share mine. Will you marry me?"

Her face lit up with indescribable joy. She flung her arms around my neck and kissed me full on the mouth for the first time in front of anyone. She laughed, cried, looked at her parents and mine, then slipped out of the chair, and knelt beside me. She kissed me, oblivious to anyone else. Then she said. "I will marry you, Jimmy Turner!"

I pulled a ring from under the footstool and put it on her finger. She stared at it. Then she kissed me again. She got up slowly and went to the table. Tears were streaming down her cheeks. "Thank you," she said first to her parents and then to mine. She started to come back to me but turned and showed the ring to her mother. After her mother saw it, she showed my mom.

My dad got up and dabbed tears from his cheeks. He lifted me up and put me in the wheelchair. Lindsey came back to stand next to me. I took her hand and kissed it.

Our reservations were for 7:30 p.m. at a fabulous restaurant complete with valet service. Lindsey hugged me all the way there. When we went into the restaurant, Chuck and Cindy were already at the table. They stood up and hugged and then everyone sat down. Lindsey looked at me for an explanation as to why our best friends were there.

"I talked to your parents after I dropped you off at the mall today. When they gave me their blessings, I called Chuck and Cindy and asked them to meet us here so you could show off your ring."

Cindy gasped. She grabbed Lindsey's hand. "Oh my gosh! Oh my gosh! Oh my GOSH! Lindsey! You're engaged!"

Lindsey gave me such an approving look that my heart tried to escape my body.

Lindsey explained what happened while Cindy and Chuck sat with their mouths open. The waiter had to clear his throat for us to notice him. When the girls left for the bathroom before the food arrived, Chuck grabbed my arm. "You are one lucky dude. And god! What a romantic!"

After we ate, Lindsey and I drove to our hill overlooking

the big city. We were so far from it that all we saw were the lights twinkling in the distance.

"I want to get married as soon as I turn eighteen," Lindsey said as I turned off the motor.

"I'd like that too," I admitted. "I was stopping here so we could talk about when."

"So enough talking, Lindsey murmured.

That is when the kissing started.

It did not turn out that we could get married that soon. Both of our parents objected immediately and rather forcefully. I had to graduate from college first and they had to have time to plan the wedding. We agreed to set the date for June, a week after college graduation next year.

The year went by swiftly. Lindsey enrolled in Tennessee U. My last year was filled with research, tests, studies and projects leaving me exhausted by the time finals rolled around.

I did not graduate at the top of my class. Too many other activities prevented that but Steve offered me the job as researcher for his medical practice. He opened his own clinic and had six doctors working for him in Nashville. He stayed with the college program so I could graduate with him as my mentor.

Steve went to Hawaii as promised but had no success finding Dr. Laird. He seemed to have simply disappeared. Without enough time and the necessary resources to track him down, Steve came back disappointed. He vowed to continue trying. In the meantime we made very little progress on our own and I was disappointed so many times that I wondered if I was going to be able to live up to Lindsey's dream, the one in which I rescued her.

My body continued to ache as my spine knitted itself together. I still had not discussed all the details with

Lindsey because I wanted it to be a surprise when I did step out of the chair and walk. I felt stronger with every therapy session. The magical day for me was when I managed to support my weight on my own feet and let go of the parallel bars a month before graduation. It was too much to hope that I would walk across the stage and Dr. Lang assured me that I was nowhere near able to do that. It might take at least another year for me to take a step. But we were both encouraged.

Graduation was awesome. I sat in the crowd of graduates and waited my turn to wheel across the stage and take my diploma in hand and wave it at Lindsey and my parents who had supported me through thick and thin. There were many tears that day! Sweetest of all were Lindsey's as we took time to ourselves—the last time we would have together until the wedding.

Chapter 15

Instead of getting married in June, we ended up pushing it back to August 15, between our birthdays.

Lindsey looked radiant on the arms of her stepfather as she walked gracefully up the aisle of the huge, packed church. Friends encouraged us from both sides of the aisle. Chess club members all sat on Lindsey's side but winked at me when I came to the front of the church in the wheelchair with my best man, Chuck Singleton and my groomsmen flanking me. I smiled back and then turned my attention to the end of the aisle where the doors were closing. My heart raced and a lump rose into my throat as the song Lindsey had chosen for her triumphant walk down the aisle rose into the air and each silvered note announced for the entire world to hear that someone special was getting married tonight.

Lindsey took my hand as her dad went to sit down beside her mother. I could not see anything or anyone else in the entire church. Lindsey was in white, pure white with the most wonderful wedding dress I'd ever seen. Her shoes were white satin and her bouquet—yeah, it was a dozen Cataleya Orchids!

Both Lindsey and I spoke our vows without help. We had memorized them from the day we met even though we did not know it. Every moment of our lives was a testimony to the vows we spoke that day. I went first.

> *"Lindsey, I take you to be my wife. I will hold you forever in my heart and with these arms. There will never be anyone who could take your place. I am so*

filled with your beauty and your love that I see no other and will never see another. If I remain in this chair for the rest of my life, it will be a place where we both will sit. If I stand someday, my first act will be to hold you in my arms. I love you from the deepest part of my heart. I will forever. I pledge this to you for now and ever."

Lindsey nearly broke into tears as she spoke her vows back.

"Jimmy Turner, you are my wholly adequate man. I could not conceive of life apart from you. I will complete you, love you, and cherish you as I have since I fell in love with you many years ago. You have my heart, Jimmy. I pledge this to you for now and ever."

The rest of the ceremony was a blur. We climbed on a plane and four hours later were driving to the beach at Destin. She had made me promise to bring her there for our honeymoon and she was glowing as she drove the rental car from the airport. We left the unpacking for morning. We could not wait to be alone.

Chapter 16

We let ourselves into the beach house. Lindsey piled the luggage on my lap and I carried it up the ramp to the porch. I put the bags down on the porch and watched as she locked the car and came to where I was waiting for her at the threshold.

"I didn't know that I was waiting for this moment all my life until right now," I said. I reached up and took her hand. "I want to carry you over the threshold."

Without the slightest hesitation, Lindsey turned and sat down on my lap. She settled in as if she had done this a hundred times before. I held her with a full heart. She was wearing jeans and a silk blouse. The fabric of her blouse slid with a whisper along my chest as she leaned back and offered me her warm, full lips. After the kiss, I reached down and powered the wheelchair across the threshold.

My earlier statement, about not having a wedding night could not have been further from the truth. This was not going to be like any other night! There was going to be one supreme difference. We would be in bed together. We could cuddle, hug, and kiss anytime we wanted to. We could look at each other for the first time. I could test the progress of my spinal cord to see if anything else had begun to come to life.

Suddenly it was awkward. We had the luggage inside the cabin; Lindsey had closed and locked the door, turned the air conditioner on and turned to face me with a look of expectation. I looked at her beautiful face and body and knew that I wanted to see her and let her see me but I did not know what to do about it.

We looked at each other for what seemed like an eternity before she leaned down and kissed me. Then she said, "Wait right here, Jimmy."

I was baffled when she walked out of the cabin and disappeared into the night. Soon I heard water running. I wheeled my chair over to the window of the bedroom that I had occupied years earlier and saw her standing below, fully clothed, with the water running. The light that had been placed there to illuminate early morning or late evening bathers was off, but she reached over and flipped it on now that she saw me at the window. After snapping the light on, she walked into the shower still fully clothed. The water dampened her hair and face. She undid the buttons on her silk blouse and removed it, letting it fall to the ground. She stood in her bra and jeans and smiled up at me. Then, I suddenly realized that she had done this before when she was thirteen. I knew that she had done it before for my benefit but I had backed away from the window that time. Now I watched as she turned her back and removed her bra. Then she turned slowly until she was facing me.

The water stopped and the light went out. A moment later, I heard her squishing across the floor to the bedroom. Then she stood in the doorway and crooked her finger at me to come.

I let her help me get undressed and into bed. Both of us ignored the wet puddles on the floor wherever she stood. When I was settled, she smiled and took off her jeans and then her panties. My heart beat crazily as she left the light on while she ran a towel across her body. Then, damp but not wet, she rubbed her hair with a towel before she slipped into the sheets and put her arms around me. I felt complete and whole for the first time since the accident.

Lindsey's eyes saw that I was physically ready for her. She touched me. "Can you feel anything down here yet?"

I could not.

She settled down and stroked my chest and face with her hand. "It won't be long now," she giggled. Then she kissed me and said, "We can wait."

We fell asleep that night more content, more satisfied than either of us dreamed was possible.

The next morning I woke up and a dream of mine came true. She was sleeping on her side facing me. Her face was beautiful in the early morning light. I reached out and moved a strand of brown hair from her face. Her eyes opened, and she smiled at me. My heart filled to overflowing.

We made breakfast and ate on the front porch as the sun rose slowly overhead. Later we would go to the beach. Sometime this morning the same company, that rented the specialized wheelchair to me a few years earlier, would be there again with the same kind of chair.

We talked of our plans, held hands, and kissed. And we kissed and held hands and talked. When we weren't kissing and holding hands and talking, we just looked at each other. Life was so rich!

When at last we came up for air, I looked lovingly at her face. I could not believe she was mine at last! I was in love with her. She had endured so much to stay with me, that I knew she loved me too. I wondered, as I looked into her brown eyes, when she fell in love with me. I could not remember asking her.

"Lindsey," I asked quietly, "when did you fall in love with me?"

The wind blew gently through the porch and caressed her hair, blowing it into her face. She reached up, slid a finger along her hairline to tuck the errant strands behind her ear. "I remember the exact moment, Jimmy." She smiled at me. Her teeth had come together nicely, without braces. She wrinkled her nose. "Do you remember the first vacation I went to Boston...the summer you got your car?"

I nodded. Mom and dad did not take a vacation that year.

"I sat in the back seat of the car, all by myself, and I missed you. I wasn't very old and we had only been friends for a year." She studied me. "Don't worry, it wasn't then. That was just the beginning of my awareness that I missed you when we were apart. I know we were friends already, but for me it was more than that."

She considered her hands while she thought. "I noticed that you were changing—no, that's not true—as you got over your anger and disappointment and began to believe in yourself, you started to become what you wanted to be."

She giggled suddenly. "I've only had a year of college and only the very basics of psychology, but I know that when you found out you had a brain, you began to unfold in ways I could only admire." She glanced away from her hands and looked into my face. "You're the smartest man I know, Jimmy. I love talking to you because we can say anything to each other without getting mad. We want to understand. Do you know how much that means to me?" She looked earnestly at me.

I shook my head but then changed my mind. "Yes," I said simply and honestly. "I think so... because I know how much it means to me."

A van drove up and shuddered to a stop. I didn't want to let the conversation die but it did anyway. Lindsey leaned over the table and kissed me before the delivery people could get out of the van and come to the door. "I love you," she whispered.

"I love you, honey." I did too. I could not fathom loving anyone else like I loved Lindsey—not if I lived to be a thousand years old.

When the wheelchair showed up, I got in and we raced to the beach. I could not wait a moment longer. I had endured months of agony to give Lindsey this gift, on this day, in this place!

We rolled across the empty, thick sand and stopped at the water's edge. The sun was at 3:00 o'clock high but not hot. The breeze off the ocean flitted through Lindsey's hair. I studied her profile as she stood looking across the endless water. I took her hand.

"Lindsey," I said. "I want you to stand right there, okay?"

She moved to where I was pointing and struck a pose. Her bathing suit was a two-piece off the rack at the department store but it would not have mattered. She made everything look good. Her eyes registered alarm as I leaned down and folded the foot rests of the wheelchair out of the way. She held her breath as I grasped the armrests and hoisted myself up. I planted my feet solidly under me and then took a deep breath. I waited until a wave washed near and retreated. Then I let go of the wheelchair.

"Oh, Jimmy!" she cried. I opened my arms to her for the first time from a standing position and she moved inside them and put her head against my chest. I wrapped my arms around her and felt the pressure of her arms on my back. We cried for joy and kissed. We stood like that until my body began to sway with the exertion and she helped me sit down.

"I have to mark this spot, Jimmy!" She looked around for something that would be permanent.

"Not really," I said. "You see that pole right there?" I pointed up the beach directly behind me away from the water.

"Yes."

"It was right here, in this spot that I told myself I would stand up and hold you on that day we came back here. It was the day after you told me you wanted to come here for our honeymoon."

"Oh my," Lindsey said weakly. She put her hand over her heart. "Oh Jimmy! I'm so glad you didn't run me off that first week."

I grinned at her. That was not the only surprise I had in store! But the second one would have to wait.

We strolled along the beach, she was barefoot and I was too. I couldn't exactly feel my feet in the sand but I could feel something—pressure, the doctor told me. The year of crawling sensations I had endured, was fully repaid when I was able to stand and hug my wife, my darling Lindsey.

That night on the porch, we recalled the exact words she had spoken and wondered how it had managed to become reality. There was so much that had happened! There were so many things working against our happiness, and us until now. I would never be sad another day in my life! I let the breeze wash over my face and wondered how I could have gotten so lucky as to have Lindsey move in next door.

We dressed for supper in rather spiffy clothes. Lindsey wanted to show me off to perfect strangers, I guess. She was in charge because she had the keys. I let her pick the place. We went into Destin and ate at the Crabby Shack. It was too noisy for me but she loved it. I loved her so I loved it too.

The phone rang and I saw on the screen that it was Steve Singleton. "Hey! Steve!"

"I hope you are enjoying your honeymoon," Steve said cheerfully. "I've got some good news for you." His voice was distant, scratchy. I checked the screen. Only one bar was showing. The signal was not very strong in this part of Florida for some reason.

"Great!" I held my hand over the phone. "Steve says he's got some good news for me." I put the phone back to my ear. The noise in the restaurant made it hard to hear. "Steve, I need to get out of the noise. Hold on." I looked at Lindsey who nodded.

Outside I put the phone back to my ear. I heard only static. I looked at the phone. It suddenly began blinking "*Out of service*". Well, good news would have to wait. I rolled back inside and saw that our food had arrived.

"Whatever it was," I said, "will keep. He said it was good news."

"Umm," she said. "This is good!" I looked at her selection. It was not something I would have chosen. I made a mental note—it was another interesting fact about this woman! In all our trips to restaurants, she had chosen conservatively. I guess she was letting down her hair, so to speak. My food was a little less exotic but tasty.

I worried about the phone call during our meal. I wondered what Steve had discovered. Maybe it was about Meckler's Disease, maybe something to do with his mentoring me. I just wish the phone had not chosen that time to lose contact with whatever tower supplied it with service!

During the drive home, I forgot about Steve. Lindsey was much more interesting.

We sat on the porch. Lindsey had helped me out of my wheelchair and onto the swing so she could swing with me. We held hands and I watched my mostly useless legs as Lindsey used her wonderful legs to push us. She leaned over to kiss me and threw up.

"Oh! I'm sorry!" She said, giggling. "I didn't even see that coming!" She got up and went to get something to clean me up. She had barfed on my lap. Thank goodness, she turned her head as it spilled out. I could feel my guts heaving a little just from the experience. Never in my wildest fantasies had *barfed on by Lindsey* made the top of the list as a honeymoon experience.

I heard her scrambling around in the kitchen and then I heard her throwing up again. I reached for my wheelchair and pulled it toward me. I swung myself into it and wheeled through the doorway into the kitchen. She was sitting on a chair at the table looking pale. Her face was drawn.

"Oh God I feel sick," she said. I avoided the puke on the floor and found a pan in the sink. I brought it to her and she promptly barfed into it. She recovered and looked at me. "I'm sorry, Jimmy."

"No! Don't be. I said for better or worse, I think. Tell me how you feel. Do you have headaches or anything?"

"I didn't until I threw up in here." I could see the pain in her eyes. She heaved again but she was empty and nothing came out. I had to look away briefly. "I need to lie down, Jimmy," she said. She held her stomach with one hand, and with the other hand, she gripped my arm. I wheeled toward the bedroom. She took the handlebars and used them for support as we went through the door and then she simply collapsed onto the bed.

I brought her water and made her drink some but she promptly threw up. Then she giggled. "I'm making a terrible wife on our honeymoon," she said.

"Hey, it happens." I took the glass back to the kitchen. I was worried. I remembered the symptoms of Meckler's Disease. Surely this was nothing more than eating something tainted! I lifted my phone to dial Steve and ask him but my hand was trembling so badly that I could not hit the right buttons.

I went back to Lindsey. She was holding her head and moaning. "Lindsey, what's the matter?"

"Bring me an aspirin, please," she moaned.

I could not bear to see her in so much pain. I got the aspirin and gave her two. She could not keep them down. In a moment, she doubled up, crying. I felt helpless, angry. Fear began to take over. I managed to call Steve's number but it rang and rang and he did not answer. I tried to think. I went back to Lindsey. She was hot and feverish. *Oh God! Do not take her from me now! Please! You know how much we have gone through! Take me instead! Please! Please!* Lindsey's premonition in New York suddenly chilled me.

I did not realize I was sobbing and crying aloud. Lindsey tried to comfort me but she doubled up again and heaved nothing. The phone rang. I glanced at the caller ID. It was Steve. Thank God! "Steve!" I practically shouted into the phone.

"Jimmy, what's the matter?" Again, the connection was lousy. I hurried through my explanation hoping he would have time to tell me what to do. "It's Lindsey, Steve! She has cramps, headaches and fever! Steve! What can I do?"

The phone buzzed with some reply but it was indistinct. I looked at it. "*Out of Service*"

"No!" I shouted. I wanted to slam the phone down on the floor and stomp it into tiny pieces! Instead, I hurried to the bed. I had to get up. I locked the brake on the chair and hoisted myself up to my feet. Now that I was standing,

I did not know what to do. I could not move forward or backward. I was so damn useless in any emergency!

Lindsey saw me standing by the bed. She gave me a pain-filled smile. "I knew you would walk some day, Jimmy. I'm glad." She closed her eyes against the pain. In my fright, it sounded like her last words on earth and she was determined to make them happy words. It was the euphoria! I groaned; hot tears slid down my cheeks.

"Lindsey, I'm going to call an ambulance," I said. I sat heavily and missed the chair. It broke my descent but scooted into the corner and I hit the floor stunned for a moment. A sharp pain raced through my back. I'd hit my tailbone. The cell phone hit the floor next to me and skittered out of my reach. I crawled over and grabbed it. I looked at the dial. It was still working. The in service light was on. I had no time to waste. I dialed 911 and held the phone to my ear.

"Jimmy, no!" Lindsey was begging me not to make the call.

"Lindsey, I have to! I can't help you, honey."

"If you do, Jimmy, they'll separate us. I couldn't bear it if this is it."

Oh God! She believed it was the onset of Meckler's Disease!

I cursed her ancestors. I crawled to the edge of the bed and reached up. Her hand was there and I held it. She was sobbing against the pain.

The phone connected and after one last look at Lindsey I told the 911 operator that I needed an ambulance and then I told them where. My phone went out of service before she could reply. I cursed the phone.

I tried repeatedly but could not get a dial tone.

"Stop it," Lindsey gasped. "Just hold me."

I dragged my weight onto the bed next to her and gathered her in my arms. She was sweaty and trembling. She pressed her face into my hair, sweat poured off her.

"Lindsey," I kissed the sweaty cheek pressed against my face. "I don't know what to do! I've got to go and get help."

"Don't!" She gasped, "Don't...leave...me...now."

I sobbed against her cheek. "Please, Lindsey! Dear God! Help us!"

She pressed her fingers into my arm. "I wanted...more than...anything...to...marry you...Jimmy. I...wanted...to...live...the...rest...of...my...life...with...you." Her stomach cramped, clamping off her words.

I couldn't lie beside her and do nothing. I started to lift my head but she grabbed me desperately. "No, Jimmy," she gasped. "Stay."

"Lindsey, I've got to get help!" I pulled away from her. She was too weak to hold me but her eyes locked onto mine. I slid off the bed and crawled toward the wheelchair. In the distance, I heard sirens wailing. I crawled back to the bed.

"I hear the ambulance, Lindsey," I said.

The sirens abruptly died outside the front door.

"Come in!" I shouted when I heard footsteps on the porch.

The door opened and a uniformed man hurried to the side of the bed. He took one look at Lindsey and opened his orange emergency box.

"99.5, BP 110 over 80, pulse 75." He spoke to the second EMT who followed him into the room.

"I'll call it in," the second man said.

He looked at me and figured it out. He got up, recovered the wheelchair, and helped me into it. "Talk to me," he said.

"She threw up just after we got back from the restaurant. She's got a rare blood disorder called Meckler's disease." I babbled, happy to have help, wanting to impart information.

"I'm going to put an IV line in." He pulled packets from his kit and turned toward Lindsey. The other man wheeled a gurney into the cabin and they loaded Lindsey onto it with expert ease. In less than a minute, they had the IV dripping saline into Lindsey's veins.

"I've got to ride with you," I said as he pushed Lindsey toward the door.

"I don't have room," he objected.

"I'm coming!"

"He has to come," Lindsey said weakly. "He can't get to the hospital." She gasped.

They barely had room to get me in but they did. They chaffed at the time it took. I wanted to hold Lindsey's hand but the attendant was working on her while he monitored her heart rate and respiration.

Lindsey's fear of separation came true when we reached the hospital. I waited in the back of the ambulance while the two EMTs took her into the emergency room. Almost immediatcly, they wheeled her out of sight. When they did not come back for over five minutes, my fear had blossomed into full-blown anger. When they finally lifted me out of the ambulance and put me into my wheelchair, I was seething.

The clerk at the desk took her time filling out dozens of forms. I told a nurse who was passing by that my wife had Meckler's Disease and that I needed to be with her. The nurse nodded and hurried away. The clerk resumed her laborious scratching on the forms. Twice she asked the same questions but I could barely answer her. My throat had constricted with the rage I felt.

When she was satisfied and I was in tears, I rushed to Lindsey's curtained-off cubicle. A doctor and two nurses were working on Lindsey. I could see Lindsey writhing in agony on the gurney. I thought suddenly of her parents. Their lack of faith in me was justified. I could not protect their daughter.

"Doctor," I said wheeling over to the bed, "My wife's dad died of Meckler's Disease. She carries the gene."

The doctor looked at me as if I had sprung a leak in my head. He was working on Lindsey. I couldn't see what he was doing. "You'll have to wait outside," he said. He looked confused for a moment. I could see him mouthing the words, Meckler's Disease as if trying to recall some obscure fact.

"Wait outside, please," he repeated. He looked at someone over my shoulder and I felt my wheelchair moving away from Lindsey. I was propelled outside the curtain as if I were a child who dared to intrude. I barely avoided slamming into the wall. When I had my chair under control, I wheeled around to see a man standing with arms crossed in front of the curtain.

"Doc says you gotta stay out." He said. He looked like he would do anything the doctor told him to.

I was ready to do battle. The look on my face must have given him second thoughts. "Look, just give the doctor a minute, please," he said quickly as I charged toward him.

"That's my wife! Let me in there!" He stepped aside thinking he would grab my handlebars as I went by. I slapped his hands away and my momentum carried me back inside the curtain. I pushed the curtain over my head and saw that Lindsey was sitting up. The doctor was looking at me. She was smiling.

Oh, God! The euphoria had hit! I looked anxiously at the doctor and at Lindsey. Her smile got bigger.

The attendant pushed the curtain aside. "Sorry, Doc, he just..."

"Its okay Cedric," The doctor said. He gave the aide a nod. "Thanks. I'll handle it."

Cedric mumbled something. He gave me a glance and then walked through the curtain.

I looked anxiously at Lindsey. I tried desperately to remember how long she had after euphoria. That meant her brain was being starved of oxygen.

"She's going to be okay, Mr. Turner," the doctor said quietly. "Just some bad food, that's all. I want to do a blood test to see for sure. She's feeling better and my guess is that she'll be ready to go home shortly."

My heart thudded. Lindsey nodded. She felt better already. The doctor had given her something for the pain and she would be drowsy for the next two hours. The doctor stepped aside and I wheeled over and put my head in her lap. She stroked my hair. I could not think and I just wanted to hold her. I wanted reassurance. "I'm such a panicky fool," I said.

"Me too," she whispered. The stomach pump had scratched her throat. "But honestly, the only symptom missing was the euphoria," she said.

The relief was like nothing I had ever felt. It was as though my body was one happy feeling from my head to as far down as I could feel. My smile was so big that my face hurt. We just clung to each other in that hospital room. We laughed and cried until the doctor asked if we needed more pain pills.

A half hour later, the doctor returned. "Listeria," he said. "The nurse will be back to give her a shot, and you should get this prescription filled. She'll be fine." He scratched on the pad and tore the sheet off. He handed it to me. "Fine honeymoon, eh?" He said sympathetically.

"It's wonderful!" Lindsey and I chorused together.

My cell phone jangled loudly. It worked just fine in places where it was supposed to be turned off! I answered and it was Steve.

"Don't hang up on me!" He said quickly. "I've found Dr. Laird. You know the doctor who did the research on the orchids. Anyway, he told me something new. He has researched twenty-two people who have this disease. The only ones to die from it are men!" He was shouting as if the phone had a bad connection. "Did you hear that? Lindsey is in no danger!"

I dropped the phone on the bed beside Lindsey and held her while I wept into her lap.

Lindsey picked up the phone and Steve delivered the news to her. When she hung up, she kissed the top of my head and said, "Let's go back to the beach. We've got a honeymoon to keep."

Chapter 17

We called for a taxi and then, while waiting, we called our parents from the hospital, waking them up in turn. Lindsey told her mom what Steve told us and added something he did not tell me. "Steve, uh, Dr. Singleton, thinks that the researcher in Hawaii, Dr. Laird, has isolated the genome that is responsible for the disease. That means in a few years they can prevent this disease from being passed on genetically!"

I told my mom and dad what happened and they were overjoyed. "That's really good news!" my mom said. My dad voiced the same sentiment. "I guess you can stop worrying and enjoy your honeymoon!"

After we hung up with our parents, we climbed into the taxi. The driver's nose wrinkled as he folded my wheelchair into the trunk and got into the front seat. "Rough night?" He asked sympathetically.

"This is the greatest, most awesome night of my life!" I disagreed happily. He gave me a look reserved for disarming crazy people and started the engine.

Lindsey and I held each other during the drive back to the white sand beach in Destin where our honeymoon cabin waited for us. We did not speak. My heart was so light I had to put my hand on my chest just to make sure it was where it was supposed to be and still beating.

I sat in the wheelchair on the sidewalk outside the cabin and patted my lap as the tail lights of the taxi faded into the distance. "There is something I've always wanted to do with you," I said to Lindsey.

She sat on my lap. Her hair brushed my cheek as she leaned back and relaxed. Despite the events of the night, I could faintly smell the shampoo in her hair and the perfume that augmented her beauty. I put my arms around the woman whose heart seemed to beat in my chest. We were one with each other. We knew each other's thoughts, hopes, fears, dreams and we were friends.

"I love this place," Lindsey said softly.

"I do too."

Her hand found my hand near her stomach and she entwined her fingers with mine. "I like you, Jimmy Turner."

"That's funny," I said, nuzzling her neck, "I like you too."

She giggled. After caressing my hand she said, "What was that thing you always wanted to do with me?"

"It's probably not what you are thinking," I said.

"Whatever it is, I'm willing."

I kissed her again. "Okay. Hold on." I dropped my hands to the outer ring of my wheels and propelled us up the sidewalk toward the cabin. Just before the ramp that led onto the porch, I turned left and muscled the chair across a small stretch of firm sand, onto another sidewalk that ran down along the side of our honeymoon cottage. I stopped under the shower spigot.

"There's something I want to know," I said. "That night, when we came here for the first time on vacation, why did you shower here that morning you went to the beach alone?"

"Why do you think?" Lindsey asked softly. There was enough mystery in her voice that I wasn't certain of her meaning.

"I don't know."

"Jimmy Turner!" She pretended to be upset with me. "Tell me the truth!"

"I know a lot of what's in your heart, but your head is still a mystery to me," I answered.

"Then tell me what was in my heart," she challenged. Her voice had softened once again.

I sat back, feeling her weight against my stomach and chest. "I think," I said after a few moments of drinking in all that she was to me now, "You wanted me to see that you were more than just brains…"

She twisted in the seat and kissed me on the lips before I could finish my sentence. When she pulled back, there were tears in her eyes. "Do you know what I see in you, Jimmy?"

"I want to know," I replied.

"Someone who wants to know me deep inside; someone I can give my heart to without fear that he will place it on a shelf as a trophy that he has won."

Tears came to my eyes along with the lump in my throat. I swallowed hard, trying to find my voice. I rested my head against the softest, most beautiful shoulder in the world because, in the end, I could not speak what was beating inside my chest.

"Do you know why I love you?" She asked softly.

I shook my head.

"Because you are beautiful inside and out to me. I can tell you anything, hope anything, dream anything and your response is always that you want to understand."

"Lindsey," I said, pulling her to my chest from her nearly upright stance, "I never met anyone like you. When I first met you, you won my respect because you saw right through my anger. After that came admiration because you…" I paused to gather my thoughts, "…because you acted consistent with your words." I shrugged. "That's the only way I know how to describe you. "You act exactly as you say." I took her hand. "And then...I saw how beautiful you were. Is it okay that I saw your outer beauty after I figured out that I loved you?"

She squeezed my hand tightly.

"Are you going to sit here all night or should I turn the shower on?" She asked after absorbing my words.

I propelled the chair forward and turned the knobs.

Lindsey undressed. When she was done, she pulled my soaked clothing off. Then she sat down on my lap and handed me the soap.

⊹-»⊹-»⊹-»

"I don't know if I can tell you how much you mean to me," I said later when we were on the porch swing. The moon was out over the water. Except for the breakers crashing rhythmically against the shore, the night was silent. A small candle burned on the glass table in the corner of the screened-in porch. It gutted and sputtered as the breeze caressed it. "But I'm going to try to do just that for the rest of my life," I promised.

I fell silent. She watched me. "What are you thinking?" She asked, touching my face with soft fingers.

I realized I was staring into the distance. "I'm doing something terribly wrong," I admitted.

"What?" She asked curiously.

"I was wondering where Cassiopeia was. I grinned wickedly at her.

She gave me a dazzling smile that told me she remembered I had said the same thing when she wanted to be serious on this very porch almost six years earlier.

"The truth, Mr. Turner," she demanded.

"I was thinking about the future."

"Why is that so wrong?"

"Because I'm on my honeymoon with the most beautiful woman in the world," I said.

"Tell me what you were thinking about that future," she said, smiling at my reason.

"I was wondering what the future held for us."

"Then that's okay," she said, "As long as it is always 'us' in that daydream."

I looked at her. We were on the porch swing. Night was around us like a soft summer quilt. Stars twinkled overhead. The sound of the surf filled my ears. The fragrance of salt filled the air we breathed.

The scent of her shampoo hung in the air between us. I loved that smell more at that moment than ever before because I had washed her hair for the first time in my life. The suds had dripped from her hair onto my chest and lap.

"It will be," I assured her fervently.

She kissed me.

I looked at her. My heart swelled like a balloon in my chest. "I can't imagine loving anyone else," I said to her.

"That's what I was thinking about," she replied, smiling. "In my future, you will."

I leaned back in order to see her entire face. She was joking. The threat of Meckler's disease was entirely gone. What reason could I possibly have for loving someone else?

She saw the confusion on my face and grinned. "I'm betting you will," she said softly.

"Are you sure you're okay?" I felt her forehead.

"Yeah, I'm fine. I was just thinking about Ashley and Robert."

I shook my head. "I don't even know them!" I protested. She was teasing me, but I could not figure it out.

"Give it about five years...I bet you'll know them then."

"Ashley and Robert?" The names meant nothing to me. I studied her face. Despite the helpful smile, she was encouraging me with I could not get her meaning.

"Or, Penny and Daniel," she said, laying her head on my shoulder. "Or, Heidi and Kory...or Lacey..."

I understood. I stroked her hair. "Our children?"

She turned her face up for a kiss. I obliged.

"Only two?" I teased, after our lips parted with a soft smacking sound.

"How many do you want?" She was serious.

"Once I get started, I may not be able to stop," I said, nuzzling her shoulder.

"Then let's get started," she said as she stood and walked into the cabin.

The end

I owe these people so much more than thanks.

Paula—You gave me the time and the space I needed to bring these characters to life. I love you.

Karen—the fact that this book has an ISBN 1-4196-6270-8 is on your head!

Penny, Heidi, Rob and Lacey—I do what I do for you—and now Bradley and Tabitha too.

Ken, Betty, Karen, Dave, Jim, Linda—Thank you for encouragement along the way.

Mom—your perfect diction and love of languages (especially English) allowed me to take a run at writing a long time ago.

Dad—you taught me the important stuff. Thanks.

Kelli, how awesome it is to get your reaction to chapter after chapter! You rock!

Then there are the folks who come in at the last moment to help. The handsome guy in the wheelchair is Adam Zachow and the beautiful woman is Kelli Roberts. Lori Z offered up the use of her wheelchair on the day of the photo shoot. [Thanks for all you do for us, Lori.]

A little insight: It took about a month to write this story and four months to edit it. The editing is by far the worst part of writing a novel. Sixty-two thousand words require the soft touch of the editor's pen. Try reading those words a dozen times! After a while, you have no idea if the story is good or bad, interesting or dull. Honestly, after the tenth time through, you no longer care! You become cranky, irritable and downright annoying to live with. That is why authors say thanks to the people around them. People who put up with their ugliness from story conception to the moment they send the final product to the publisher. Then we become better people to be around...for a week or two...until the next story starts bouncing around in our heads.

Poor Paula—I owe her the most loving thanks imaginable. Sometimes I would rush into the bedroom, having just been with Lindsey and Jimmy through some horrible or exciting time of their imaginary life. I was liable to blurt out what terrible thing had just happened in my literary world. Paula would be sympathetic until she realized she was expending emotional energy on an imaginary event. Nothing had really happened to anyone "real." For all that unnecessary trauma you endured, thanks!

Other Stories by RC Waggoner

Saving Crystal
Crystal's Story